CHRISTMAS IN MY HEART

4

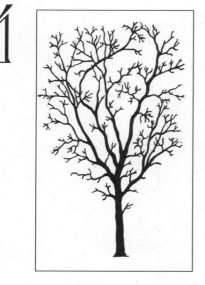

JOE L. WHEELER

REVIEW AND HERALD® PUBLISHING ASSOCIATION
HAGERSTOWN, MD 21740

The author assumes full responsibility for the accuracy of all facts and quotations
as cited in this book.

This book was
Edited by Richard W. Coffen
Designed by Patricia S. Wegh
Cover illustration by Superstock/Currier & Ives
Typeset: 11/12 Goudy

PRINTED IN U.S.A.

99 98 97 96 95   5 4 3 2

R&H Cataloging Service
Wheeler, Joe L., 1936-   comp.
    Christmas in my heart. Book 4.

    1. Christmas stories, American.   I. Title:
Christmas in my heart. Book 4.
            813.010833

ISBN 0-8280-0993-7

Dedication

Collections 1, 2, 3, and 4 are dedicated to my beloved
"Once Upon a Christmas" Mother—
Barbara Leininger Wheeler

Acknowledgments

Introduction: "A Pennsylvania Deutsch Christmas," by Joseph Leininger Wheeler. Copyright 1995. Printed by permission of the author.

"Trouble at the Inn," by Dina Donohue. Reprinted by permission from *Guideposts Magazine*. © 1966, by Guideposts, Carmel, NY 10512.

"Christmas at Wittenburg," by Gladys H. Barr. Published in *Upward*, December 23, 1956. Printed by permission of Thomas Barr (on behalf of the Barr family) and the Southern Baptist Sunday School Board.

"And It Was Christmas Morning." Author and original source unknown. If anyone can provide knowledge of the authorship, origin, and first publication source of this old story, please relay this information to Joe L. Wheeler, care of Review and Herald® Publishing Association.

"Joey's Miracle," by Hartley F. Dailey. Copyright © 1995. Printed by permission of the author.

"Christmas in the New World," by Rosina Kiehlbauch. Printed by permission of the American Historical Society of Germans from Russia.

"Charlie's Blanket," by Wendy Miller. Copyright © 1995. Printed by permission of the author.

"A Day of Pleasant Bread," by David Grayson (pseudonym of Ray Stannard Baker). Published in *ADVENTURES IN FRIENDSHIP*, Doubleday, Page & Co., 1910.

"Unlucky Jim," by Arthur S. Maxwell. Printed by permission of D. Malcolm Maxwell and the Review and Herald® Publishing Association.

"Christmas Day in the Morning," by Pearl S. Buck. First published in *Colliers*. Copyright © 1955 by Pearl S. Buck. Copyright renewed.

"Pink Angel." Author and original source unknown. If anyone can provide knowledge of the authorship, origin, and first publication source of this old story, please relay this information to Joe L. Wheeler, care of Review and Herald® Publishing Association.

"Christmas Lost and Found," by Shirley Barksdale. Reprinted with permission of *McCall's Magazine*. Copyright © 1988 by Gruner & Jahr USA Publishing.

"A Doll From Muzzy," by Penny Estes Wheeler. Copyright © 1995. Printed by permission of the author.

"Truce in the Forest," by Fritz Vincken. Used with permission from the January 1973 *Reader's Digest*. Copyright © 1972 by The Reader's Digest Assn., Inc. Further reproduction strictly prohibited.

Contents

The Lamb

Little lamb, who made thee?
Dost thou know who made thee,
Gave thee life and bade thee feed
By the stream and o'er the mead;
Gave thee clothing of delight,
Softest clothing, woolly, bright;
Gave thee such a tender voice,
Making all the vales rejoice?
      Little lamb, who made thee?
      Dost thou know who made thee?

Little lamb, I'll tell thee;
Little lamb, I'll tell thee.
He is called by thy name,
For He calls himself a Lamb;
He is meek and He is mild,
He became a little child.
I a child and thou a lamb,
We are called by His name.
      Little lamb, God bless thee!
      Little lamb, God bless thee!
        William Blake (1757-1827)

A Pennsylvania Deutsch Christmas

Joseph Leininger Wheeler

With this fourth collection I'd like to take you on a journey with me, as exciting a journey as I've ever taken: a journey into my own past.

Actually, it all started last summer when I attended my first ever Leininger family reunion, held in a very old Lutheran churchyard in the Blue Mountains of Pennsylvania. Even though my branch of the family had moved west well over a century before, I was still welcomed as warmly as if our absence had been only for a few months. And strange as it may seem, though we came from far and near, from local families and from families that had moved away generations ago, yet we shared common interests—even resembled each other! I was so moved by the experience that I determined to find out more about my German roots.

As fate would have it, sitting next to me at that reunion was one of my distant cousins, Richard Leininger Pawling, who is a specialist in living history; in fact, he takes his shows on the road. And one of his specialties is Pennsylvania Deutsch—not Dutch—history. Indeed, there never was a Pennsylvania Dutch region of Pennsylvania, only German. Yet centuries later, most Americans still insist on labeling this heavily German region "Dutch"! When my newfound cousin discovered my own interest in Christmas traditions, he promised—and followed up on it—to send me a packet of Pennsylvania German Christmas history. Later on the editors of the American Society of the Germans from Russia, in Lincoln, Nebraska, sent me another. Out of this treasure chest of Christmas history I have been able to make possible our joint journey into the past. It is my fervent hope that many of you will wish to go back, with your families, to this rich heritage every Christmas from now on.

German migration really started with the Hessian mercenary troops the British brought to America to defeat General Washington's armies. Instead, in one of the pivotal moments of the war, on Christmas Eve of 1776, Washington and his armies crossed the icy Delaware River to Trenton, New Jersey, where they surprised the Hessian troops who, true to their roots, had celebrated Christmas with much cheer—and spirits—and were thus easily routed. Well, after the war, the Hessians decided to stay. They wrote home. The Germans came. And came. And came. Eventually, they would represent more than one-third of America's population. Today, two centuries later, few of us would not have at least some German blood flowing in our veins, hence these Pennsylvania Deutsch traditions belong to us all!

In spite of their drubbing on the Delaware, they

liked it there, eventually returning Washington's favor by commandeering that part of the East Coast we label "Pennsylvania Dutch" country. From there they exploded across the continent, many in the Conestoga wagons they made.

And wherever they went, they brought their traditions, Christmas and otherwise, with them. What an incredible loss for us all it would have been had they never come to our shores!

Louis Prang and the Christmas Card

In the Prussian city of Breslau was born, in 1824, a frail child named Louis Prang, destined to become the king of Christmas cards. Early on he fell in love with print design, wood and metal engraving, dyes, and color processing. After working for a time in his brother's paper mill in Westphalia, he moved on. His internship in the craft of printing included stints in print and dye operations in the Austro-Hungarian Empire, Switzerland, France, and Great Britain. During those years not only did he learn his craft inside and out, but he also became more and more obsessed with art, never happier than when he was studying the old masters in galleries throughout Europe.

In 1848 the common people rose, seemingly in unison, and challenged virtually every throne in Europe. Louis Prang fled to America, arriving in New York on April 5, 1850. Shortly thereafter, he moved to Boston, where working for Frank Leslie, he became a master engraver, then a master lithographer.

By 1856 he was in business for himself, and in 1860 organized Prang & Company. In 1864, as the Civil War raged across America, Prang returned to Europe to study art firsthand again. When he returned, he set out to master a process by which every American could own great art. By 1866 he had developed a technique he called "chromo" (lithographic copies of art). So successful was he that in 1867 he was able to relocate to Roxbury, Massachusetts, with state-of-the-art equipment. He was one of the first printers to use color—in fact, it was his use of color on business cards that set the stage for Christmas cards.

At the Vienna Exposition of 1873, Prang's life was changed by meeting Mrs. Arthur Ackerman, the wife of his agent in Britain. She had the foresight to suggest that he capitalize on a phenomenon which had begun in England during the 1840s, the Christmas card, and blitz London with dramatic multicolor cards.

Prang wasted no time: his vividly colored cards hit British shelves in time for the 1874 holiday season and were bought up by an entranced audience. Earlier (in 1868) Prang had introduced illuminated chromos of Christmas scenes for hanging on American walls, but now he decided to launch something much bigger: a virtual revolution in American holiday observance. In 1875 his multicolored Christmas cards became the smash hit of the season. Each year that followed, he expanded the line (including flowers, birds, butterflies, nativity scenes, angels, winterscapes, elves, and Santa Claus). Inside were poetic lines penned by such literary luminaries as Longfellow, Whittier, and Bryant.

Production of these cards quickly soared into the millions. Ever since then, Christmas cards have helped to define the season. So in all your hauntings of flea markets, garage sales, bookstores, and antique stores, make a special effort to search out those lovely works of art: the cards and prints of Louis Prang. (I am deeply indebted to Peter E. Stevens' *The Mayflower Murderer and Other Forgotten Firsts in American History*, William Morrow and Company, New York, 1993 for this fascinating story.)

Christmas Season

Anchoring this family festival was the Advent. On the first Advent Sunday, four weeks before Christmas, a large Advent wreath with a red candle is hung. On each successive Advent Sunday another red candle is added—and for each day, a paper star. On one side of each star is written an Old Testament verse; on the other side one from the New Testament. All the children in the family memorize each day's verses.

They also brought their counterpart of the Twelve Days of Christmas—except that Germans, perhaps because their nights were longer, called them the Twelve Nights of Christmas. Shakespeare's *Twelfth Night* play reflects the broad acceptance of the night aspect in Europe.

And while Germans might differ mightily over doctrine (most were either Lutheran or Catholic), they disagreed hardly at all on the Christmas traditions they loved.

In Germany on every December 6, St. Nicholas Day, a Christmarket (or fair) would begin. The streets would be filled with Christmas activities and with families flooding the narrow streets and buying cookies, candies, trees, and toys from booths along the way.

Christmas Eve for them was a deeply spiritual family time, a time to attend Christmas services where they listened to music, the gospel story, their children reciting memory verses, etc. Everything possible that could be done to make it a children's festival was done.

Christmas was not a commercial season in those days, because they emphasized Christ and giving rather than self-gratification and excess.

According to Alfred Hottle's *1001 Christmas Facts and Fancies* (A. T. De La Mare Co., New York, 1938), December 24 has traditionally been such a family day in Germany that even restaurants are closed so everyone can be home. On Christmas Eve after families return from church, Mother supervises the decoration of the tree, the setting up of the *Krippe* (Christmas crib), and perhaps even the installation of a musical holder for the Christmas tree.

December 26 was considered a second Christmas and would be a time filled with talk, visiting neighbors and family, sleigh rides, games in house and barn, dances, and courtship. Outside, fences would be decorated with seasonal greenery, and on the door a Christmas wreath, crowned by a hunting horn.

The Christmas Tree

It was in the city of Strassburg in 1604 that we have recorded the first use of the Christmas tree. However, both before then—and after—it was not uncommon to bring fruit trees indoors in order to induce them to bloom during the Christmas season. Ever since 1604, the Christmas tree has been an integral part of German Christmas observance. When Prince Albert of Saxe-Coburg married Queen Victoria, he brought the

Christmas tree tradition with him.

Martin Luther, seeking ways to make Christmas especially meaningful to his children, not only adopted the nativity observances but also the Christmas tree. According to German tradition, wandering through the woods one serene Christmas Eve, Luther was filled with childlike wonder, gazing transfixed into the star-filled night. After a time he cut down a small snow- flocked fir tree and set it up at home for his children. Since he could not bring the stars down, he substituted candles on the branches. (See "Christmas in Wittenberg.")

German immigrants brought the Christmas tree to the New World. For Germans in forested America the tree was an absolutely essential Christmas ingredient. "Bringing in the Tree" was an annual tradition the whole family looked forward to. First of all, both permission to cut, and the blessing of the landowner, had to be secured.

So what happened when there weren't any trees to be found? That was a very real problem to Germans who lived in the vast treeless steppes of Russia or the Great Plains of America. In both cases, the absence of the tree from daily life only enhanced the power of it as a symbol. People for miles around would journey to see the "Tannenbaum" (majestic evergreen) brought into the church from some distant forest; there the children would gaze upon it with awe.

Inside homes there would most likely be not only a tree in the parlor but also a tree in each of the other downstairs rooms, as well as a tree in each of the bedrooms upstairs. These trees would be decorated (naturally, the family's main tree the most lavishly adorned) with homemade strings of popcorn or cranberries, chains of brightly colored paper, gilded pine cones and locust seed pods, gold and rose ribbons, honesty plant, Queen Anne's lace, curly pretzels, dried apple rings, gilded nuts, shepherd's crooks, and tiny baskets. Cookies of every shape imaginable, candy canes, and rich red apples hung on lower branches within easy range of children.

Decorating the tree was looked forward to with anticipation all year long. Upstairs in the attic there would be trunks full of decorations and ornaments, most all handmade and many generations old. Among them would be molded red, blue, and saffron glass balls (many made in Germany), which could reflect tiny points of light from the wax candles. These heirloom decorations, needless to say, were among the most cherished of a family's possessions.

The tree was dedicated to the Christ Child and thus was taken very seriously. It was *not* a secular addition to the season. In fact, invariably—just to make sure this truth was never lost sight of—on the very top would be the Christmas star and just beneath it the Christmas angel.

Christmas Putz

Another appealing Germanic tradition is that of the putz (from the German verb *Putzen*, signifying "to decorate or enhance in beauty.") According to Pennsylvania Deutsch historians: "The American custom of erecting a putz seems to have originated with the Moravians but the custom long ago spread to non-Moravian households. Essentially, the putz is a landscape, built on the floor or on a table or portable platform. As a Christmas feature, it existed before the advent of Santa Claus or the American Christmas tree, and almost invariably had the creche as its focal point. The starting point for the construction was an irregular terrain of hills and valleys, covered with moss brought from the woods before a heavy frost and stored in a damp place. A mirror served as a lake, paths or roads were of sand or, in later years, colored sawdust. Evergreens' branches were converted into trees in scale with the rest of the putz or, if the whole creation was in miniature, ground pine, known locally as Jerusalem moss, made very convincing six-inch-tall trees. Driftwood, lichen-covered bark, and mossy stones from a brook were used for creating caves. Cardboard or wooden houses were set up as farmsteads or villages; human figures, in scale, went about their business of tilling fields or whatever the putz-maker chose to represent. A church putz would concentrate on background for the figures and appurtenances of the manger scene, of course" (*The Goschenhoppen Newsletter,* Green Lane, Pennsylvania, December 1985).

Food!

While German cuisine needs no introduction, even so at Christmas housewives have traditionally outdone themselves. Should you have strayed into a German kitchen with its midnight black stove shining with bright nickel trim, your olfactory sense would have been overwhelmed by cooking fragrances such as cinnamon, cloves, allspice, citron, lemon, ginger, mint, vanilla, and almond paste.

Sandtart, springerlie, marzipan, lace, and ginger cookies would take form from heirloom tin cookie cutters, producing birds, rabbits and other animals, fish, stars, angels, tulips and other flowers, etc. Also there would be stick-to-the-ribs mincemeat pies, cringele, eider kringle, lebkuchen, fruitcake, glazed pound cake, pfeffernüsse, honey cake, as well as gingerbread men and animals that would end up on the window sill. Combined, these fragrances represented a time of year when body and soul communed in perfect harmony.

Christmas Eve Legends

One of the most intriguing Christmas practices had to do with summer rainfall predictions. If you put out of doors on Christmas Eve three salted onion slices—representing the unpredictable growing months of June, July, and August—then invoked the blessing of the Trinity, on the morrow when you examined for moisture content, the dampest slice would foretell which month of the new year would be wettest. In some cases 12 (one for each month) would be put out.

Another tradition that children have loved has to do with farmyard animals: that, on this holy night, are given special powers. It was believed that if a farmer went to his stable with his Bible and a lantern on this eve and began reading the Bible at 8:00 p.m. and continued until 11:00 p.m.—all the while eating a piece of bread with salt sprinkled on it—that during the following hour he would be able to understand what the animals were saying. It was also believed that at precisely midnight Christmas Eve the animals would kneel.

13

Stille Nacht

And what would Christmas be without such Germanic contributions as "O Tannenbaum," "Away in a Manger," Mendelssohn's "Hark! The Herald Angels Sing," the fifteenth century's *Est Ist Ein Ros* ("Lo, How a Rose E'er Blooming"), and that ultimate Christmas carol, *Stille Nacht* ("Silent Night")?

"Away in a Manger," although not even a German hymn, has been determined to be one anyhow by myth-makers. For better or worse, it seems, it will always be known as "Luther's Cradle Hymn." Since it was known that Martin Luther sang his children to sleep, it was therefore imagined (by someone long ago) that this lovely hymn could well have been the one he crooned.

The story of *Stille Nacht* has been told many times, but one of my favorites is that told by Father Richard, of the Old Santa Barbara Mission many years ago: "The organ of the little church of Arnsdorf near Salzburg, Austria, had in the last days before Christmas become unfit for further use. Mice had eaten at the bellows, and this seriously troubled the parish priest, Father Josef Mohr. He went to his organist and school master Franz Gruber and expressed his disappointment, saying, 'We must have something special for midnight mass.'

"On the day before Christmas Eve of 1818 the Father was called to administer the last rites to a dying woman. It was late when he returned. Pausing on a height overlooking the town he fell to musing. The snowy mountains loomed above him and below in the valley the dark outline of the village could be discerned. Here and there a faint light glimmered in the dark, and over all was that vast stillness so peculiar to the wide open spaces of Nature. Suddenly, the good man murmured, 'It must have been something like this—that silent, holy night in Bethlehem.'

"Powerfully affected, he hastened home, sat at his desk and wrote. Late at night he paused, read over what he had written, then read it again:

1

Stille Nacht, heilige Nacht,
Alles schläft, einsam wacht,
Nur das traute, hochheilige Paar,
Holder Knabe im lokkigen Haar,
Schlaf in himmlischer Ruh,
Schlaf in himmlischer Ruh.

2

Stille Nacht, heilige Nacht,
Hirten erst, kund gemacht,
Durch der Engel Halleluja,
Tönt es laut von fern und nah,
Christ, der Retter ist da,
Christ, der Retter ist da.

3

Stille Nache, heilige Nacht,
Gottes Sohn, O wie lacht,
Lieb aus deinem göttlichen Mund,
Da uns schlägt die rettende Stund'
Christ in deiner Geburt,
Christ in deiner Geburt.

1

Silent night, Holy night,
All is dark, save the light,

Yonder where they sweet vigils keep,
O'er the Babe, who in silent sleep,
Rests in heavenly peace,
Rests in heavenly peace.

2

Silent night, peaceful night,
Darkness flies, all is light;
Shepherds hear the angels sing.
Alleluia! Hail the King,
Christ the Saviour is born,
Christ the Saviour is born.

3

Silent night, Holy night,
Child of Heaven, Oh how bright,
Was thy smile, when Thou wast born,
Blest indeed that happy morn,
Full of heavenly joy,
Full of heavenly joy.

"—It pleased him and he thereupon retired to bed. Arising next morning, he took up his manuscript, reread it, hastened to his friend Franz Gruber, and read it to him. As soon as Franz Gruber read the lovely words, inner voices seemed to fill his humble quarters with an angelic chorus. Indeed, he caught the true spirit of the hymn. He sang it to his wife, and in the hushed silence that followed, she said, 'We will die—you and I—but this song will live.'

"At Christmas Eve midnight the organ did not sound in the church at Arnsdorf. The congregation indeed felt a lack of it—until with Father Josef Mohr singing and Franz Gruber playing his guitar, the hallowed strains of 'Silent Night' fell upon their ears, and the echo of the first rendition of this holy hymn has not died away in the world, even now, at the conclusion of over a hundred years. The congregation sat enthralled; no organ, no— but a special gift has been given to the Christ Child on His birthday" (*1001 Christmas Fads and Fancies*).

Der Belsnickel and der Christkindel

For many years now I have wondered how one of America's cultural icons, Santa Claus, came to be. Especially did I wonder how such a secular figure could have evolved out of such a Christlike churchman as St. Nicholas. And then I came across two of Germany's most significant contributions to Christmas: the *Belsnickel* and the *Christkindel*, born in the Valley of the Rhine and shadowed by the alpine heights where Germany, Switzerland, and France meet.

What especially intrigued me about these two Germanic figures is that they account for one of the most inexplicable qualities of Santa Claus—his omniscience, his godlike ability to know everything about you: seeing you when you are awake or sleeping, knowing when you've been bad or good. In short, possessing a power never attributed to St. Nicholas himself.

Both Catholic and Lutheran Germans brought *Christkindel* and *Belsnickel* across the Atlantic with them. Apparently their long-ago ancestors felt St. Nicholas was an inadequate motivational figure for their children. Hence they split him in two: on one side, the purity, innocence, and beauty of the Christ Child, known as *Christkindel* (also as Christ Kind, Christ Kindly, and later, as Kris Kringle); and, on the

15

other, the dark, punishing, and rather demonic *Belsnickel*, who brought retribution and terror with him. Apparently Luther had been concerned because he felt the cult of St. Nicholas was getting out of hand, almost preempting Jesus. Thus his support for these "new" Christmas intermediaries.

The role of *Christkindel* was generally given to a girl, one who was attractive, blond, had a pleasing voice, could articulate well, and possessed an engaging sense of humor. In most cases, she would be dressed in white, with a red sash around her waist, a veil over her face, and a gold crown on her head. She would carry a bundle of switches (or sticks). Usually she would be accompanied by an entourage of young girls (often arrayed in fantastic-looking costumes). She or one of her company would carry a sack of nuts and candy. Her basket would contain toys.

Although the term *Christkindel* meant Christ Child, it was a bit misleading because in reality she was a hybrid of the Christ Child, the Christmas angel, and the ancient Germanic folk heroine (or good fairy) known as Hertha (sometimes Bertha, the Hearth Goddess, or the White Lady, who guards German children). As the days would become shorter and the season of the Advent neared its end, children could hardly contain their eagerness for the coming of the *Christkindel*. During this period, if the sun would set in a bright red sky, parents would tell them that the reason for the scarlet sky was that the *Christkindel* was baking cookies for those children who had been good during the year.

The *Christkindel*, later on Christmas Eve, supposedly would return when all were asleep and enter the house through such openings as an open window, a keyhole, the fireplace (rarely), or through the walls, and would place the gifts on the table—*not* under a tree!—in the Christmas room. Although it was known that she came donkeyback or muleback with great light around her, no one ever was privileged actually to see her during these deliveries of presents and coins.

Some farm households each Christmas Eve would leave hay outside for the animal that had the honor of carrying the Christ Child. On Christmas morning the hay that remained—blessed also by the dew of that holy night—would be fed to the animals on the assumption that it now held special powers and would fortify the animal for the coming year.

Inside the house children would place empty plates on tables or window sills, with the expectation that if they had been considered good, *der Christkindel* would leave them something special. If they had not, then they would get whatever *der Belsnickel* felt they deserved—most likely a chunk of coal.

On the stairs—as is done on Day of the Wise Man, January 6, in many parts of the world—children would place their shoes (cleaned and polished) on Christmas Eve, hoping *der Christkindel* would fill them with nuts, candy, and that rarest of delicacies for nineteenth-century children—an orange. (Note here the substitution of shoes for Hertha's slippers.)

So angelic was the *Christkindel* that it is easy to see why her visits were perceived as spiritual ones. The time varied but usually it would be Christmas Eve, after the lamps were lit, that one of the *Christkindel*'s companions would ring a bell in front of the window. Then after establishing contact with those inside, the question would be asked: "May the *Christkindel* come in?" Answered in the affirmative by the lady of the house, the entourage would enter and almost immediately the *Christkindel* would begin grilling the children as to their behavior during the year.

Not surprisingly, children would often be frightened by all this commotion. They would be asked standard questions such as "Have you obeyed your parents all this year?" "Have you said your prayers every night?" etc. If they had been good, they were rewarded with gifts. If they had been bad, they'd receive blows or be switched. Some *Christkindels* would affect great doubt about the regularity of their prayer life, causing all the children to fall on their knees and recite their prayers as proof of their assertions.

If there were children who had misbehaved—usually recalcitrant boys—a signal would be given that would summon *der Belsnickel*. Almost invariably—in the early days, at least, before degeneration set in—the two traveled together. *Der Belsnickel* would usually be a strong male with a deep booming bass voice. He would be covered by a shaggy fur coat (often with the fur worn on the inside). Generally he would either wear a grotesque mask or his face would be blackened with burnt cork. On his back would be a long chain that rattled terribly when he wished to frighten, and in one hand a bundle of switches. Oftentimes he'd wear patchwork clothes—everything he wore or carried was of antique vintage—and carry a large bow and a quiver of arrows. Attached to his long coattails would be bells. His stockings would be of green buckram, on his feet

would be Indian moccasins, around his ample waist a wide belt, and on his head would be an ancient hat worn low over his forehead. His old clothes would be ill-fitting, so pillows often would exaggerate the already well-nourished figure. If he was beardless, he would most likely don an artificial one; above it would be his trademark: a sinister upward-curving horned moustache.

He or an associate would carry a large feedsack in which to stuff bad boys and carry them away—usually no farther than a snowbank in the vicinity. Another sack or basket would hold the gifts for those who had been good.

Actually, *Belsnickel* is a corruption of what he had been called in Europe—*Pelznickel*. *Pelz* in German means "fur or pelt," and *Nickel* a shorter form of "St. Nicholas." But there is a darker aspect as well, for the original meaning of *Nickel* also encompassed "fur demon," "fur imp," and a devil-like aspect.

In portions of Germany he was called *Pelzmartel* (in honor of Martin Luther), and his visit was tied to Martin Luther's birthday on November 10. In other parts of Germany, *der Pelznickel* came on December 6, the Eve of St. Nicholas. In yet other parts of Germany were rival figures with very similar characteristics, such as *Knecht Ruprecht*, *Hans Trapp* (even more gruesome looking than *der Belsnickel*), and *der Christmann* (Father Christmas)—an impressive white-clad figure who combined the roles of *der Christkindel* and *der Belsnickel*.

Unlike his gentler counterpart, he rarely deigned to ask if he could come in but stormed into the house like an avenging demon, rattling his chain, shaking his bells, and making fierce noises no one could understand. Bad boys would usually cringe in terror, but there was no refuge for them. Custom dictated that even brothers or sisters would propel the erring ones forward to be punished with voice, switch, or lash.

Every child knew he'd be coming, and awaited his arrival with a curious mixture of eagerness, dread, and outright terror. On Christmas Eve they knew his onslaught was imminent by the sound of his bells, the rattling of twigs across the window, a rude knock, and the thumping of his booted feet on the stairs.

In remote villages *der Belsnickel* would sometimes attract the children by slamming open the front door. He would throw handfuls of nuts and candy on the floor, and then after children would scramble after his bait, pounce upon them, wielding whip and sticks right and left indiscriminately, on the basic premise that the unrighteous deserved it and the righteous weren't as righteous as people thought they were!

The secret of his (sometimes, however, the *Belsnickel* was a woman) omniscience was known to the adults, because he was in reality usually a neighbor, friend of the family, or close relative such as an uncle or grandparent. Such a relationship guaranteed inside knowledge of behavior, secrets known only to family members, personal idiosyncrasies, frailties, etc., which made his (or her) pronouncements and questions so terribly dreaded. Even good children shook to their core, wondering which of their hidden sins would be found out.

When he had stomped up the stairs into the parlor, the family would be waiting—the older children huddled in corners, the baby on Father's lap, and the next smallest either hiding behind Mother's skirt or cowering under her apron.

Without any preliminaries, immediately the inquisition would commence:

"Have you said your bedtime prayers every night?"

"Have you memorized all your Sunday school verses?"

"Can you repeat the catechism?"

"Have you been naughty?"

"Did you play hide and seek near the furnace—as you were warned not to?"

"Did you faithfully do your chores every day?"

"Did you snitch any charcoal from the charcoal house?"

"Did you mistreat your little sister?"

These were not merely general questions he asked. They got very specific and personal. And some of the *Belsnickels* would carry big black books with them, and inside would be written specific misdeeds that would be incorporated into the grilling:

"Did you or did you not, last October, deliberately let out of the corral Widow Schmidt's favorite milk cow, Old Bossy?"

"Weren't you the one who pushed over the outhouse two weeks ago, knowing full well the schoolmaster was in it?"

Or for a child who professed good behavior:

"That won't do! Last year you promised not to sleep in church. And just last Sunday night, you embarrassed your entire family by snoring. *By snoring!*"

He would often make them recite poetry or Bible verses they had learned for the Christmas program in the church. And many children were so petrified with fear that not a word could they remember.

When there was erring to be punished, *der Belsnickel* would flail out with his long lash—often making more noise than inflicting pain—or rap on the head, back, hand, etc., with the switches.

After the grilling was over, he would toss down on the floor pieces of candy, nuts, etc. and roar with laughter as the children fought each other for pieces.

As a matter of fact, through it all, he laughed . . . a lot. And it was funny—to the adults. Well, not always. Not when he severely reprimanded Father for failing to keep the harness well greased, the horses properly shod for winter's icy roads, or the snow shovel in its proper place. Neither was Mother exempt. Woe unto her if she had failed to keep the dishes clean or the furniture dust free!

Once the serious part was done, *der Belsnickel* distributed the goodies he had brought with him: toys, oranges, apples, and transparent candy in the shape of toys. At that time, his job done at that house for the year, he would often reveal who he was and take refreshments. In fact, as a result of the punch some of the home-brewed holiday cheer packed, some of the *Belsnickels* were reprehensibly lit before they finished at the last house!

Just as was true with the *Christkindel*, the *Belsnickel* too had another job to do that night, returning when all were asleep to punish the bad and reward the good. He it was who supposedly filled stockings, hats, caps, and the Christmas boxes that were set apart just for him.

In later years as Americans became more secular and the old traditions lost their force, Belsnickeling became merely a form of Christmas roistering. More masks were sold at Christmas than at Halloween as gangs would flood the urban areas with hilarity. Many would perform music, with and without instruments, "mumming" at each door for treats, a Christmas tradition that got so out of hand in England that Puritan leaders banned all Christmas celebration during the Commonwealth period. On Christmas Eve the streets would be filled with revelers out for fun and mischief, costumed as bandit chiefs, Indians, clowns, harlequins, devils, demons, ragamuffins, minstrels, and performers, etc. Many, having had far too much to drink, made the night hideous with kettle drums, trumpets, penny whistles, cornets, violins, bones, and tambourines.

The institution of *der Belsnickel/der Christkindel* survived for about 150 years in America before being swept aside by that department store import, Santa Claus. In a later introduction we will explore his fascinating evolution through St. Nicholas, the *Christkindel*, the *Belsnickel*, Moore's "Visit of St. Nicholas," Christmas cards, and Thomas Nast's famous cartoon in *Harper's Illustrated Weekly*.

* * * * *

The Fourth Collection

Each year that passes, it seems, contributes to how much of the tent of my life the Christmas camel has taken. One thing is certain, the camel appears intent on getting all the way inside!

The frequent book signings represent a very special time to me, because they give me a unique opportunity to meet so many of you face to face. And I also welcome the opportunity, provided by my inscriptions, to become part of the fabric of your family life.

As many of you know, Dr. James Dobson sent out, as part of the Focus on the Family Christmas messages of 1993 and 1994, Dr. Frederick Loomis's "The Tiny Foot" and Cathy Miller's "Delayed Delivery" (both included in the second collection). Many of those who read them have written to thank me—*and* to scold me for making them cry. If the truth must be told, unless a story moves me deeply, chokes me up, it never makes it into *Christmas in My Heart.*

For this fourth collection, you voted in a number of stories by personally speaking with me, sending me favorite stories, or by asking me to seek out a story you've been looking for. You might be interested to know that each time such a suggestion is made, one of four things occurs: (1) I begin searching for the story, (2) I make out a folder for it and place it at the bottom of the pecking order, (3) I fall in love with it and raise it toward the top without the usual multi-year process, or (4) I follow usual procedures—move the file folder forward each time one of you gives it your blessing.

As you can see, you have a major say in the process. And blessings upon so many for sending me copies of their favorite stories! It's truly amazing how out of many versions I am able to salvage one fairly accurate version of a special old story. Each one often fills in a missing piece (text, authorship, where published previously, when first published, who holds the copyright, etc.) Without such continued transfusions, it would be impossible to keep the *Christmas in My Heart* series going for long without compromising story quality.

The stories you voted in? "Trouble at the Inn," "Christmas Day in the Morning," "Truce in the Forest," "Jolly Miss Enderby," "Unlucky Jim," "And It Was Christmas Morning," "Christmas in the New World," "Pink Angel," "Christmas, Lost and Found," and "Roses in December."

I have taken occasional editorial liberties, updating words or terms that have become archaic or have acquired negative connotations. In a few rare instances, I have left out terms or phrases that I felt did a disservice to the whole.

Coda

I look forward to hearing from you, and please do keep the stories, responses, and suggestions coming. And not just Christmas stories. I am putting together collections centered around other genres as well. You may reach me by writing to:

Joe L. Wheeler, Ph.D.
c/o Review and Herald® Publishing Association
55 West Oak Drive
Hagerstown, MD 21740

Trouble at the Inn

Dina Donohue

What could be new about a local nativity play? Children in bathrobes and sheets flubbing their lines. . . . Not always. Sometimes this very spontaneity results in the sudden need to wipe something out of one's eyes.

Simple though it be, short though it be, this little story is the hands-down write-in winner of the year! Many have begged that it be included.

For years now whenever Christmas pageants are talked about in a certain little town in the Midwest, someone is sure to mention the name of Wallace Purling. Wally's performance in one annual production of the Nativity play has slipped into the realm of legend. But the old-timers who were in the audience that night never tire of recalling exactly what happened.

Wally was 9 that year and in the second grade, though he should have been in the fourth. Most people in town knew that he had difficulty in keeping up. He was big and clumsy, slow in movement and mind. Still, Wally was well liked by the other children in his class, all of whom were smaller than he, though the boys had trouble hiding their irritation when the uncoordinated Wally would ask to play ball with them.

Most often they'd find a way to keep him off the field, but Wally would hang around anyway—not sulking, just hoping. He was always a helpful boy, a willing and smiling one, and the natural protector, paradoxically, of the underdog. Sometimes if the older boys chased the younger ones away, it would always be Wally who'd say, "Can't they stay? They're no bother."

Wally fancied the idea of being a shepherd with a flute in the Christmas pageant that year, but the play's director, Miss Lumbard, assigned him to a more important role. After all, she reasoned, the Innkeeper did not have too many lines, and Wally's size would make his refusal of lodging to Joseph more forceful.

And so it happened that the usual large, partisan audience gathered for the town's Yuletide extravaganza of the crooks and crèches, of beards, crowns, halos, and a whole stageful of squeaky voices. No one on stage or off was more caught up in the magic of the night than Wallace Purling. They said later that he stood in the wings and watched the performance with such fascination that from time to time Miss Lumbard had to make sure he didn't wander onstage before his cue.

Then the time came when Joseph appeared, slowly, tenderly guiding Mary to the door of the inn. Joseph knocked hard on the wooden door set into the painted backdrop. Wally the Innkeeper was there, waiting.

"What do you want?" Wally said, swinging the door open with a brusque gesture.

"We seek lodging."

"Seek it elsewhere." Wally looked straight ahead but spoke vigorously. "The inn is filled."

"Sir, we have asked everywhere in vain. We have traveled far and are very weary."

"There is no room in this inn for you." Wally looked properly stern.

"Please, good innkeeper, this is my wife, Mary. She is heavy with child and needs a place to rest. Surely you must have some small corner for her. She is so tired."

Now for the first time, the Innkeeper relaxed his stiff stance and looked down at Mary. With that, there was a long pause, long enough to make the audience a bit tense with embarrassment.

"No! Begone!" the prompter whispered from the wings.

"No!" Wally repeated automatically. "Begone!"

Joseph sadly placed his arm around Mary, and Mary laid her head upon her husband's shoulder and the two of them started to move away. The Innkeeper did not return inside his inn, however. Wally stood there in the doorway, watching the forlorn couple. His mouth was open, his brow creased with concern, his eyes filling unmistakably with tears.

And suddenly this Christmas pageant became different from all others.

"Don't go, Joseph," Wally called out. "Bring Mary back." And Wallace Purling's face grew into a bright smile. "You can have *my* room."

Some people in town thought that the pageant had been ruined. Yet there were others—many, many others—who considered it the most Christmas of all Christmas pageants they had ever seen.

Christmas at Wittenberg

Gladys H. Barr

Martin Luther towered over his age as did no other, matched in religious history perhaps only by the Apostle Paul. Luther was a robust man who never did a half-hearted thing in his lifetime, a man so obsessed with the brevity of a mere lifetime that he rarely slowed his breakneck pace.

Four and a half centuries later, Luther-related scholarship continues at an unrelenting pace. One can count on the fingers of one hand the people in history who have generated such undying fascination.

But once in a while—certainly at Christmas—he did slow his footsteps. This moving little story details such a moment. Like so much that has been written about this greatest of Reformers, it is difficult, if not impossible, to separate legend from history. However, since his selfless generosity and the loving support of his wife Ketha are a matter of record, it is felt that Barr's account is in character and true to life.

(Gladys H. Barr [1904-1976] spent considerable time in Europe, studying in the Martin Luther archives. Out of this came her fictional biography of the great Reformer, Monk in Armor, *published by Abingdon-Cokesbury Press in 1950. She also wrote biographies of John Calvin [The Master of Geneva]* and John Bunyan [The Pilgrim's Prince], *both published by Holt, Rinehart & Winston.)*

For additional information on Luther, see "A Pennsylvania Deutsch Christmas."

The wind blew like a blade, and the small, quiet streets of Wittenberg were deserted. Martin Luther smiled, a little wryly. All sensible people were shut away safely indoors, their purchases made, gathered with their families around the warmth of the hearthstone with the odor of good baking in the air, wrapped in the happiness and security of this Nativity Eve of 1537.

But it was a beautiful night, perfect for the eve of Christmas, with the fresh, clean snow mounded in the crooked streets and the thin, bright stars so far overhead. He enjoyed walking. A professor spent too much time indoors, he thought, although he liked his work. Teaching young people, enjoying their companionship and their vigor, was exciting to him. It was his lifework. But tonight—tonight it was good to walk alone under the stars.

As he walked, his right hand clutched tightly at the flat wallet that Ketha, his wife, had given him. It held one gulden—the last coin from the sale of their cow. Tonight it would buy toys and goodies for Hans, Magdalene, and little Martin. Ketha seldom allowed him to spend money for such things, but then—tomorrow was Christmas Day.

The sound of singing broke into his thoughts. It was

the voice of a boy who stood in the yellow light pouring from Frau Carlstadt's windows, in the house next to his own.

The voice was clear and good; and Martin stopped still at the sound, his mind flying back to visions of another boy, almost forgotten in the passage of the years. He felt his throat muscles tighten as he stood in the shadows, watching, listening, remembering. The first boy had been a student, and he, too, had begged for bread. There had been doors which opened grudgingly, doors which had never opened at all. There had been nights when that boy had gone to bed too hungry to sleep. He understood.

Now this singer was turning away. This was one of the unopened doors. For an instant Frau Carlstadt's head appeared etched against the yellow candlelight inside. Then it vanished. The boy moved on with drooping shoulders, pausing before the next house to begin his song again. With a smile and a blessing, a plump serving maid in a blue cap and dress thrust the heel of a loaf of bread through the doorway. Hungrily the boy lifted the bread to his mouth.

He turned swiftly as Martin, his mind resolved, approached him. He would do for the boy . . . whatever he could. He knew the deep-set eyes and the gaunt face with its mop of red hair. The boy was one of his own students, Paul Göelichter, a first-year student at the University of Wittenberg. Paul had already attracted the attention of the faculty, he remembered, because of his unusual scholarship.

Paul recognized him. "I could not go home for the festival, Dr. Luther," he explained in a low voice. "I . . ."

"I understand," Martin said gently. "Come, Paul. We will carol together. I'll teach you the new song I've written for my own children."

For more than an hour they sang together.

Away in a manger
No crib for his bed
The little Lord Jesus
Lay down his sweet head. . . .

The little city of Wittenberg was not rich, but Martin knew that the townspeople knew and liked him, and he was grateful for it now. They were good. And the song was like a magic tune opening their doors. Paul had fruit, an onion, a leg of mutton, bread.

Now lights were dying along the narrow streets, and as the last candle disappeared, Martin saw that the stars were suddenly very cold and far away. He felt his teeth chatter, and his fingers and toes ached. He saw that Paul was shivering, too, as he pulled one foot and then the other from the snow. They must go home.

At the corner where his way must part from Paul's, Martin hesitated.

"Thank you, Dr. Luther." Paul smiled at his small sack.

Slowly Martin opened his wallet, his numb fingers fumbling with the coin Ketha had entrusted to him.

"You must have this," he said, thrusting it into Paul's red, unmittened hand. Paul held it up and stared. He lowered his head and stood for a moment with his shoulders hunched, unspeaking.

"Dr. Luther," he said finally, "you are very kind.

Thank you for your Nativity gift. I shall never forget your friendship."

As he watched Paul hurry away, a strange emptiness swept Martin. The last gulden was gone. There would be no Nativity now for Hans and Magdalene and Martin. And Christmas was a child's day. There would be only a few playthings he had made in his carpenter's shop—a parchment angel with outstretched wings for Magdalene, a roughly carved replica of the Nativity scene, and some wooden animals for the boys, and his new song. That was all.

Martin turned slowly toward the Black Cloister, where Ketha would be waiting eagerly for him and the gifts she trusted him to bring. Would she blame him now for the children's sakes? She had said always that he was too generous with his small store when there were three children of his own.

She was right. The happiness that had flooded his heart at Paul Göelichter's gratitude was gone. Wearily, he trudged toward the monastery gate.

There, he stopped involuntarily. The moon and stars covered the newly fallen snow with silver. Their light, falling on the branches of a fir tree, illuminated the crystal night, shed a glory that must, he thought, be like that glory which had shown on that first Nativity Eve. If he listened tonight, he might transport himself across the centuries, hear the angels' song, join the shepherds, and kneel at the very feet of the Christ child. Above the fir tree's spire he saw a star gleaming more brightly than all the rest, and his eyes fixed upon it.

If only the children could see that tree, the sky sown with stars, and the brightest above it! It made no

difference, he realized, that the gulden was gone. This tree was a symbol of the real meaning of the Nativity, a gift lovelier than all the gifts of earth. He felt his heart begin to sing again. His children must see the tree. With quick steps he went to his barn, found his ax, and came back to the tree.

He was nailing a board to the bottom of the tree for a stand when there was a sharp rapping at the door. Frau Carlstadt stood in the entrance to the common room, scowling at him.

"Come in, neighbor," he beamed at her. "Come and see what I have for the children!"

"I came in only to borrow a candle," she snapped. "All this hustle and bustle over the Nativity! I have no time for it!"

"But you must wait! Come, now. . . ."

The frau's stiff old face was set. "Such idolatry will bring down the wrath of God upon you," she told him, "and you should know, Dr. Luther, that it is wicked to waste firewood. Now what are you doing with that angel and those wooden animals?"

"The angel will decorate the tree," he said gently. "There'll be a crèche at the foot and a star at the top, and candles, tied to the branches. Don't you think it's beautiful?"

"It looks like some pagan invention for a festival!" she answered him.

"But you do not understand!" He smiled at her. "Christ came to light our world. To me, for Christians everywhere, these branches hold that light tonight."

Frau Carlstadt shook her head stubbornly. He watched her select a candle from the rack near the door

and bounce out, muttering to herself about the foolishness of men and the wastefulness of the season. If she felt this way about the tree, what would Ketha say?

He shifted uncertainly toward the cookhouse. Ketha had been bustling about inside all day. She would be tired, and when a woman is tired she is prone to anger.

"What took so long? Where have you been, Martin?" Ketha's voice, low and strained, sounded suddenly from the doorway.

He drew a deep breath and turned to face her. "Ketha, I've done it again," he said directly.

"Oh, no, Martin!" she whispered. "Martin, not tonight!"

He faced her, his elation gone, fumbling for words to tell her of Paul Göelichter and the memories of himself, long ago, that had flooded him tonight. "He was so hungry, Ketha!" he finished, but she was no longer listening.

She was circling the tree. She turned to him suddenly, her small oval face breaking into a smile. She rushed to hug him to her heart.

"Martin, Martin!" she cried. "In all the world there is no man as kind as you . . . or half as wonderful!"

"I'll help you, Martin," she said when he released her. "It will be the finest Christmas the children have ever had."

Climbing on a stool, she tied the parchment angel on the tree. Its dress was of silver brocade. They found small candles to glimmer on every branch, and finally, together, they placed the star at the very tip of the fir. It had been a glorious evening, and Martin fell asleep.

Dawn had hardly crept through the diamond-paned window when Ketha shook him.

"Come," she whispered, her eyes bright with excitement. "We must make ready for the children!"

They tiptoed to the bottom of the stairs, where he found a faggot, lighting first the fire on the common room hearth, then each white candle, watching a warm glow spread over the gray walls. "I almost thought I saw the angel's wings move," he told Ketha, and they laughed understandingly together.

"O, Papa!" Hans' excited voice came from the doorway.

Martin went to lift Magdalene, carrying her to the tree as tiny Martin toddled after them.

"Papa!" Magdalene gasped. "Oh, Papa!"

The baby squealed and clapped his fat hands, and then, suddenly they were all quiet. The lowing of cattle in a stable somewhere outside, the crowing of a rooster, the rumble of a cart in the distance, were the only sounds in the stillness.

"The hope of the world," Martin explained slowly, "is here, my children. This tree is the symbol of the rich life that God promises to those who love him. Angels still summon sinful men to Christ. In a world of violence, here alone is man's peace."

"Put me in a chair by the fire," Magdalene whispered. "I want to sit and look at it, Papa."

He set her gently by the fire. "While you look at the tree, think about its meaning, and I shall tell you a story."

He told them about Paul Göelichter and of what he had done with the money for their gifts. They looked quietly at the tree as he spoke, and then they were still.

Magdalene was first to break the silence. "There's something you forgot, Papa," she said gravely. "You didn't invite him to come to dinner."

"I think that can be remedied." Ketha smiled at her children as she moved to Martin's side and slipped a warm hand in his.

Looking down, he saw that his wife's eyes were shining and tender. It was the same look she had given him when they had made their wedding vows more than 12 years before.

"We may not have money, Martin," she said, "but we have things far more valuable. We have a Christian home. The children have a good father, and I have a husband who loves me." She drew a deep breath. "What more could a woman want?"

"I deserve no credit for loving you, my Ketha," he said softly. "As for money—at the Nativity season when we have no money, we'll always have a fir tree."

"Whether we have money or not, we'll always have a fir tree," she corrected him.

"We'll always have a fir tree," young Hans echoed as he danced around the lighted tree with Martin toddling after him. They clapped their hands and shouted joyously, and Magdalene's bell-like voice blended with her brothers'. "We'll always have a fir tree," they sang. "We'll always have a fir tree!"

And It Was Christmas Morning

Author Unknown

Priorities. Each life is built on them, consists of their varied order. Always has, always will. In this old story, two women within the same extended family prioritize their family relationships differently—at least they did before a certain Christmas Eve. This is a wonderful story, one that moves me deeply every time I read it. I have been saving it for this special fourth collection.

To learn more about barn animals on Christmas Eve traditions, see "A Pennsylvania Deutsch Christmas."

Christmas was a week away, and everything was ready.

"Isn't it joyful, Peter," said Peter's mother.

"Yes," Peter's voice lacked enthusiasm, "and now let's talk."

"But, my darling, I haven't time. I must telephone to Mrs. Madden about the old ladies from the home who are going to dine with us Christmas Day, and I must talk over my menus with Martin. And Daddy will be here before we know it."

"Well," said Peter, resignedly, and got out his Noah's ark, and set the animals all in a row on the rug in front of the fire.

The rug was a velvety, deep-piled thing, with honey-colored lights. Peter liked to think of it as the sands of the desert. When the animals walked on it, two by two, the camels and leopards and all the lions, the effect was tremendous. Peter was, of course, too old for Noah's ark. He was 7 and he went to school. But he loved his Noah's ark in the same way that he loved the great log in the fire, and the sound of the wind booming about the high and handsome apartment house in which he lived; and in the same way that he liked the shine of the candles in the dining room, and the smell of the roast meat for dinner.

His mother sat at the telephone and told Mrs. Madden things in the same words that she had told them to Peter.

"Isn't it joyful, Maude? I have everything ready except wrapping the parcels, and Peter is going to help me with that! We are tying them with blue, sprinkled with silver stars. We are so tired of red. And the blue gives a hint of the Madonna idea. Yes? Oh, there will be 10 of us—we three, and the two old ladies from the home, and big Peter's brother, Robert, and his wife and three boys. No, we are not going to have a tree."

Peter picked up his ears. His mother hadn't told him that. No tree. No thick spicy fragrance of pine, no spiny branches that grew brittle as the days went on and strewed the waxed floor with needles like the ground in the forest.

"Mother," he said, as she hung up the receiver, "why didn't you tell me that there won't be any tree?"

"Oh, did you hear? Well, you've always had a tree and I thought of something new. It's a secret. But, darling . . ."

Peter knew that tone. His mother's logic would be convincing. They never quarreled. Peter had had it impressed upon him that quarreling wasn't well-bred. His polite protests always ended in acquiescence. He was not in the least afraid of his mother, not physically afraid; but he grew so tired of her eternal rightness. Although, he wouldn't have called it that. There never seemed to be any room for his own ideas.

So he dropped the subject and set three camels out on the honey-colored rug. Martha, the cook, had come into the dining room, which was just beyond the library, and was talking to his mother. There was second-maid, Lulu, setting the table, and she stopped to listen to his mother's instruction.

"I am making my lists up, Martha, so that you can put in your order early."

She read the menus, and Peter, traveling with his camels over the sandy desert on a magical quest, was aware of an appetizing succession of foods, from which he mentally picked out his favorites—candied sweet potatoes, and Marie-Louise soup. He liked the name of that soup so much that he had always eaten it in spite of its rather complicated flavor. His father had shown him a picture of Marie Louise.

"If you have any suggestions, Martha, let me know now. The color scheme will be green and white. I'll order the centerpiece from the florist, Lulu; there'll be mistletoe for the big silver bowl, and tall white candles. And the canapés must be green, Martha, and pistachio ice cream in Christmas-tree forms . . ."

The drowsily-listening Peter was aware of the cut and driedness of it all. They had turkey every other Sunday in winter, and canapés and ice cream were not novelties. He didn't know what he wanted. But there was a picture in a book of a pudding all in flames. And his father had read to him about the Cratchits and of how their pudding bobbed in the copper. His mother's bright voice stopped. Martha went back to the kitchen; Lulu came into the library and pulled the chain of the lamp. Then she went on to other lights and duties. Peter lay on the rug and dreamed. The camels loomed large through his half-shut eyes. Three kings were riding them, in turbans and long robes. Then someone said in a hearty way, "Asleep, Peter?"

Peter sat up. "Hello, Daddy. No, I wasn't. I was waiting for you."

"Good boy." Big Peter's eyes fell on the three camels on the honey-colored rug. "It's a good thing," he said, "that you started them so soon. They have far to travel."

"Yes, they have," said Peter. His hands stole into his father's. To his mother the three toy camels would have been just three toy camels. To Daddy they were gold and frankincense and myrrh. They sat and talked together until Mother came in. She was dressed beautifully, in a gown that looked like a flame.

"Oh, Daddy," she said, with a sort of shining reproach. "Are you here? I thought every minute you'd be coming up. It's so late and I had an early dinner because of the play."

"Are you going out?" Daddy got up and kissed her.

"I told you this morning—the Russians."

"I remember. Is dinner ready?"

"In 15 minutes. I was a bit late myself. I have to fit everything in. These are busy days."

It seemed to Peter, weighing it, that his father's days were busy. He looked after people's eyes—a specialist. But he never talked about being in a hurry. "Want to come with me?" he asked Peter, and Peter followed him to the upper rooms of their spacious apartment, and watched the swift 15 minutes of transformation, which began in a quick shower and ended with a dress coat.

While the shower was in progress, Peter gazed out of the window. "It's snowing," he mused, and when his father came back, "and the snow is funny where the light shines on it."

His father, a fascinating figure in his fat bathrobe, and with hair wet and rumpled, took time to look. "It makes me think of an old melodrama I saw when I was a boy, Peter.

"There was paper snow, and it came down on the heroine in just one spot—a handful or two—and the rest of the stage was clear—"

Peter adored his father's reminiscences. He wanted to ask more questions about the heroine out in the snow. But his father warned him. "I am in no end of a rush. Save it up, old chap, and we'll talk about it after dinner. It was a corking old play. Two orphans."

Peter went downstairs, hugging within his heart the thought of that paper storm . . . two orphans—and why was one of them out in the cold . . . ?

After dinner: "Tell me about it, Daddy."

And Mother asked, "About what?"

"Oh, said little Peter, "something he saw at a play."

"Darling, he hasn't time. It is late as it is. And the car is waiting."

Big Peter laid his hand on his son's shoulder, "Lucia," he said, "must we go?"

"Of course. We're ready." Then the car was announced, and they went away, and Peter sat by the fire and waited for Lulu, and wished that his father was there to tell him about the orphan in the paper snow.

Big Peter's office had a succession of rooms like the sections of a telescope. You began with the great reception halls, and ended with Big Peter's tiny private office. Only special patients came into that very end room. Big Peter always opened his morning mail there and read as much of it as he could before people came to him about their eyes. And it was the morning after he had been to see the Russians in a strange and moving play that Big Peter had a letter from his only brother Robert. It would be, Robert said, utterly impossible for him and Joan and the boys to come down for Christmas. It was a great disappointment to them all, but that was one of the things which happened now and then to a country practitioner. One of his patients would need him on the twenty-forth, and he and Jean had talked it over and had wondered if Big Peter and Little Peter and Lucia couldn't come up to the farm for a glorious old-fashioned Christmas Day dinner "such as you and I had when we were boys together."

Big Peter was a successful man. He and his brother, Bob, had studied medicine together, and when their father had died and the money was divided, Bob had decided to go back to the hills and take up his father's practice. Big Peter, then, had thought him foolish. The city promised so much. And he was not tied to things as Bob was tied. Even now, as he rode safe and warm in his closed car, Bob might be floundering through great drifts, up there in the hills.

Yet, up there in the hills, life was simpler; perhaps after all Bob had the best of it. Big Peter wondered what had happened to his own life—and Lucia's. Lucia was lovely. One couldn't pick a flaw in her. Yet she seemed separated from him by some intangible barrier. And she was separated, too, from Little Peter. It was noticeable how the boy shut her out of his confidence; how he left all the close and intimate things to say to his father when they were alone. And a boy shouldn't . . . a mother was a mother. Big Peter remembered his own . . . a serene person, who would sit with folded hands and an attentive gaze while he poured out his heart to her.

Little Peter had never been to the farm in winter. With his father and mother he had spent several weeks there one summer. Lucia had not liked it. She was city-bred. She had always lived in a perfectly ordered home. Big Peter adored her, but he admitted reluctantly that at times her perfections clicked like busy machines. That night he and Lucia dined out. Little Peter saw them off. "Don't you like her in that dress, Daddy?"

"Yes, it is your loveliest gown, Lucia."

She laughed a little. "You two—you are as alike as peas! I wonder why this gown takes your eye?"

"I know why it takes my eye," said Little Peter, gravely. "It is like a buttercup."

"It is like a whole field of buttercups," said Big Peter.

And Lucia just laughed again and said, "Gracious, a field of buttercups sounds as big as—hoopskirts!"

It was late when Lucia and Big Peter came home from their dinner party, and it was while they sat in the library where the fire had burned down to ashes and an open hearth, that Big Peter said, "I had a letter from Bob."

"When are they coming?"

"They are not coming, Lucia. Bob has a case that will hold him over to the twenty-fifth. They want us to come up for the weekend and eat Christmas dinner with them."

Lucia, in the field-of-buttercups gown, leaned back against the dark leather of her chair and said, "Well, of course, we can't."

"Why not?"

"You can't get away, can you?"

"Yes. McGreager will look after my patients."

She considered that for a moment. "But all our plans are made. We have so many engagements. It will be impossible to break them."

"I should like to make it possible."

She enumerated patiently. "We have accepted an invitation for the Stacy's dinner, and the Lorings, and Muriel Abbott is giving a dance, and . . ."

He lifted his hand. "Let's get away from all of them. Little Peter would love it."

"But I have everything planned for Peter, too. A surprise. I have asked a lot of children to come and sing carols, instead of a tree. And Peter will give them presents from a huge Christmas pie."

She argued it and he listened, his eyes fixed frowningly on the fire. Usually he let her have her own way. He had, like Little Peter, learned the futility of argument. Lucia could everlastingly prove her point. And she was always so disturbed when he lost his temper. He did not mean to lose it now. He felt that Peter ought to have a tree. He, himself, wanted it. It seemed to him a breath of his own pine woods. He was always sorry when New Year's Day came, and the tree had to be taken down. He and Little Peter made a ceremony of burning it in the fireplace. "You see, it goes back up the chimney," he had told his small son, "and the wind carries it away to the forest."

And now Lucia was saying, "Jean and Bob are great dears and the boys are darlings. But their house is terribly haphazard."

He brought himself back to her. "Oh well, of course. If you feel that way about it, we won't think of it." He stood up. "Let's go to bed. I'm dead tired and tomorrow is my day at the hospital."

She, too, stood up. "Perhaps Little Peter can go to the farm in the spring," she said, in her bright voice, "when we haven't so much on here."

"I wasn't thinking entirely of Peter. I was thinking of . . . myself."

"Would you really like it?"

"Like it? Yes. Why, it was home to me when I was a little chap." He found it hard to go on.

Her fingertips caressed the lapel of his coat, the field-of-buttercups gown was like sunshine against the black.

"We'll go, of course. I'm not so selfish."

He was eager. "Lucia, you'll adore it. You've never seen anything like its charm in winter."

They went upstairs together, his arm around her. And he was half-apologetic. "It is too bad that you'll have to spoil your plans."

Yet the last apologetic impulse died, when before going to bed, he went in and looked at Little Peter. The child was as warm and rosy as his own pink pajamas. He had crisp brown curls and the firm set of his chin was like Big Peter's. As the father drew up the covers, there was a rustle under his hand. Little Peter had written a note on his very own paper, with a fat gold "P" at the top. Big Peter read it under the lamp.

"Dear Santa: Please bring me a tree. Mother says I am not to have one. So will you just drop it down the chimney—there isn't any fire before 7 in the morning.

Yours truly, Peter Blake"

Well, Peter should have his tree. They would have a wonderful holiday. Big Peter went back to his wife. She had taken off the yellow gown and was wrapped in something thick and warm and fur-trimmed.

"You look like a white pussy-cat," he told her.

"Do you like me, Peter?"

"I love you."

It is one thing, however, to agree to a plan of which you don't exactly approve, and it is another thing to adjust yourself to it. Little Peter's raptures when he heard of their trip to the farm puzzled his mother.

"But how do you know you are going to like it, Peter?"

"Well, Daddy has told me about it."

"You may not like it as well as Daddy did."

"Yes, I shall, Mother. Father says I can sit in the kitchen and watch Aunt Mary make doughnuts and sprinkle them with sugar when they come out of the fat. He used to do it when he was a boy."

"But darling, you know you are not allowed to eat doughnuts."

"Well, Daddy said I might, up there. He said if I walked a lot and cut down Christmas trees that even doughnuts wouldn't hurt my tummy."

"Did he say that you could cut down Christmas trees?"

"He said I could help." Little Peter's cheeks were scarlet with the excitement of it all. Lucia sighed. She wished that Big Peter wouldn't upset her diet arrangements for her son. She was having a great many notes to write and explanations to make over the telephone. It seemed best to say that Big Peter needed a rest. She told that to the Lorings and the Stacys and to Muriel Abbott. They were all very sorry for her. Maude Maddox agreed to take the two old ladies from the home off her hands. The children who were to have sung the carols were given a little party on the day before Peter went away. The whole thing was perfectly managed, and all the mothers praised Lucia. After everybody had gone home, Little Peter was very polite about it. "They had a nice time, didn't they, Mother."

She was moved, unexpectedly, to ask, "Did you?"

Truth got the better of politeness, "Not so very."

"But why not, Peter?"

"Oh, it was like all the other parties, Mother."

She stared at him, a little frown fretting her forehead. His words were an echo of his father's as they had driven home one night from a country club party. "They are all alike, Lucia. And nothing seems real."

She had wondered then what he meant by "real." As for herself, she had been chair of the committee, and things had really been very well done. And everybody had been pleased except Big Peter, who called it "artificial" and "cut-and-dried."

"It would have been hopeless without cocktails."

"But you didn't drink any, Peter."

"I never do. And neither do you. Yet you seem to get a lot out of it."

Lucia was quite sure that Big Peter ought to get a lot out of it, too. But he didn't, and now here was Little Peter!

She packed their bags with warm things, thick sweaters and underwear.

"I can't have my two Peters taking cold," she told them, "and those old country houses are apt to be freezing." She need not have worried, however. Uncle Bob's house was warm enough. Little Peter felt that it was warm not only to your outside feelings, but to those inside of you. You went straight into the lamp-lighted front room, and there were three cats on the hearth. The fire was back of them and the cats looked black. But when you came up to them they were three colors—one was a bright and beautiful yellow, one was gray, and one was black.

Little Peter took the yellow cat on his lap. "I haven't had one since I was here that summer," he said to his Aunt Jean.

"There are more of them out in the barn."

Little Peter felt that he could sit there forever with

that warm, fat pussycat in his arms. But his mother was saying, "May I put Peter to bed? It is so late for him."

"Doesn't he want something to eat?"

"We had dinner in the dining car, Jean."

"But I do want something to eat, Mother."

"Peter!" Then gravely, "Well, a glass of milk," and Peter put down his cat and went with his aunt to get it.

They had to walk down three steps to the dairy; and there, around the wall of the broad shelves, were pans of milk and all the room was sweet with the smell of it. And the floor was painted yellow, just the color of the cat, and the cream was yellow. And there was a dipper and a glass. When he drank his milk, Little Peter talked to his Aunt Jean. He didn't feel shy, and he liked the way she listened. She seemed to put her mind to it, as his father did.

"We haven't any cats," Little Peter told her, "or any animals."

"Our pets are just part of the family. There's Old Caesar. He goes everywhere with your uncle, and the people know the dog as well as the doctor . . . and there's young Brutus who watches the house. And there's Tessie, and the old tortoise-shell pussy. She keeps her kittens at the barn. And it is always a great ceremony when she brings them up to be fed. We all go out to see them. And she is so proud!"

"At home," said Peter, "I have my Noah's ark, but of course the animals are not alive."

"Still," said Aunt Jean, understandingly, "they are a great help. You can play they are real."

"That's what I do." Peter found himself telling about the camels on the honey-colored rug. "Three kings . . ."

Aunt Jean nodded. "Do you know," she said, and Peter thought she was a very beautiful lady in her blue linen dress, with her shining hair and attentive blue eyes, "do you know I have often wondered what the animals thought when they first saw the Child."

"They fell on their knees," Peter elucidated.

She smiled, "That's just a legend, isn't it?"

"Well, Daddy says some people believe that they kneel down on Christmas night. Do you believe?" Little Peter had finished his milk, and he handed the glass to Aunt Jean. "Thank you," he said. Then, carefully, "They might kneel, you know."

He tucked his hand in hers as they went up the three steps together. He felt that he had had a very wonderful visit with Aunt Jean in the milk room. And they were very well acquainted. It was as if he had lived with her all his life.

The two days before Christmas were tremendously interesting to Little Peter.

It was a joyful adventure to get up early and help feed and water the stock, and watch the milking with uncle Bob's three boys. Their names were Oliver and George and Theodore. Little Peter's mother thought that the boys names should have been different. "Why didn't you carry on the family line?"

Aunt Jean smiled. "We decided to start a new one. We don't intend that our boys shall ever blame their ancestors for anything. We want them to think about their descendants."

"How queer!" said Little Peter's mother.

"Well, it does sound queer," said Aunt Jean, "but they have three big names to live up to and they seem to like it."

The boys drove a fat little horse into town every morning to school. But the fat little horse was now having his holiday with the rest of them. He went up in the woods to help bring back the tree. Little Peter rode on his back part of the way. His father walked beside them, and the snow sparkled, and all the lovely young pines saw it and said, "Isn't it better to die as a Christmas tree than to be mown down in a storm to the ground?"

And later, Peter's father said to Uncle Bob, "That's the trouble in town . . . he has no contact with reality. Out here, among all the living things, life and death take on their proper proportions. I don't want him to shrink neurotically from the thought of pain and poverty and dissolution. I want him to accept them as a part of things—unafraid."

Getting ready for Christmas in Aunt Jean's kitchen, Little Peter found a great event. One didn't just telephone to the butcher and baker and confectioner and have things quite magically brought to one's back door. Aunt Jean and her Swedish maid, Olga, baked the pies; and the turnips and potatoes and onions were brought up from the shelves of Aunt Jean's pantry. And the turkey! But that was the tragedy! The turkey came right out of a beautiful flock, all shining bronze, that Peter had seen in the sunshine! And Peter had to be consoled. Peter sat in the kitchen, and watched Aunt Jean make the mince pies. He thought the coal range much nicer than the gas range at home. The fire glowed in it and it gave out warmth and its great ovens baked loaves and loaves and loaves of the loveliest bread.

He liked the way, too, that Aunt Jean and Olga served the meals. They had two courses, and there were great platters of meat . . . and everything was on the table at once except the dessert. And Uncle Bob said grace, and the grace he said was this: "O Lord, make us strong men and good men, and strong women and good women. For Christ's sake, amen." And he said this three times a day.

It seemed to Little Peter that one just had to be strong and good when one heard things like that three times a day in Uncle Bob's hearty voice.

He talked it over with his father. "Why don't you say it at our house?" Little Peter was polite. "Oh well, of course. Yours is nice, . . . but Uncle Bob's sticks in your mind."

There was one thing that Big Peter had promised. They were to go out to the barn at midnight on Christmas Eve; there was a chance, Little Peter had said, that the animals might kneel.

"You mustn't be disappointed if they don't," his father told him.

"Well, I won't. It's just a legend," he said, quoting Aunt Jean, "but then, you know, Daddy . . . they might."

Peter found that while Aunt Jean was a very busy woman, she was not busy in the way that his mother was; she always seemed to find time for her boys and for Uncle Bob. When they came in, she would drift to the fire and the chintz chair, and sit there while they told her the news, or asked her opinion, or relieved their minds of some burden of thought. And at night she sat by the fire and knitted while the boys read aloud, or Uncle Bob told them all of his day's work.

"She reminds me," said Big Peter, "of my mother."

"She reminds me," said Lucia, with unexpected spite, "of a tranquil cow," and tried to laugh it off.

But he couldn't quite, and Lucia couldn't laugh either. And for a long time they were silent, and at last she said, "I don't know what is the matter with me to say a thing like that."

But the thing that was the matter with Lucia was jealousy, although she didn't know it—jealousy, green-eyed, jaundiced.

And she was jealous of Aunt Jean. At first she hadn't been. She had felt superior. And self-satisfied. She knew that she was prettier than Aunt Jean. And better dressed. And her house was well-ordered. And Little Peter's manners were perfect. And for the first few hours after she arrived, she had quite wanted to patronize Aunt Jean, and to tell her how to do things; how to run her house like clockwork, and how to teach Olga to wait on the table, how to manage Uncle Bob so he wouldn't say that odd grace. And she had felt that all that food on the table at once was a mistake.

People didn't eat that way anymore. Not so heartily and heavily. There could be less informality, more exquisiteness; Jean was carrying simplicity to excess.

But after two days of it, Lucia began to feel that perhaps Jean was wiser than she had seemed. For Aunt Jean was like a sun around which her small world revolved. Her boys adored her. Her husband adored her. Bob never came in from his rounds without shouting, "Where's Jeannie?" and greeting her as if they had been parted for ages. His eyes shone for her. He was her comrade, her lover.

As for the boys: to see them at her feet while she knitted—young Ted's rough head against her knee, the light in Oliver's glance as it met hers, the affectionate assurance with which young George demanded her opinion and got it—was to see a queen in her own domain. And Lucia was not a queen. She was rather, a dictator. But Peter and Little Peter did what she wanted them to do. But they did it listlessly. At times they seemed to draw away from her. More and more they talked together, shut her out. As for her competency, didn't it consist merely in making up lists and ordering other people to do things? She had expert maids. She couldn't make a dress. She couldn't cook a meal. She couldn't sweep a floor or keep a set of books. And Jean could do all of these things.

But that didn't matter. The thing that mattered was that Jean was the sun who lighted her own small world. Lucia envied her that. Of course, being a sun in a city apartment presented some difficulties. She wondered what Jean would do if she lived in town. She made up her mind to ask her.

It was the night before Christmas. The tree was set up in the living room, and there was the thick, spicy smell of it, which Little Peter loved. And late in the afternoon, Little Peter and his cousins had popped corn while the snow came down outside and they had strung it into chains, and while they had strung the chains they had talked about names. He felt that it must be very interesting to know that you were Oliver-Cromwell Blake and George-Washington Blake, and Theodore-Roosevelt Blake.

"I am just Peter," he said. "Like my father and grandfather."

"No," said Aunt Jean, who was knitting in her chintz chair. "You are Peter not only like your father and grandfather, but you are like Peter the rock."

"Who was he, Aunt Jean?"

"Read about him, Oliver."

So Oliver read from a big shabby book, "Thou art Peter, and upon this rock I will build my church; and the gates of hell shall not prevail against it."

And Peter, listening, felt tremendously thrilled. Not that he quite understood. But he understood enough to know that Peter of the rock must be rather splendid to be named for, far more splendid even than Cromwell or Washington or Roosevelt.

Then Lucia, who was sitting back in the shadows said, "Jean, I don't see how you do it."

"Do what?"

"Make yourself one of them."

"It is easy enough," said Aunt Jean, "if you take time for it."

Lucia wanted to say, "How can one take time in a city apartment?" But just then Uncle Bob came in, and Big Peter, and Uncle Bob had to have his supper at once. He was called out on a case, and Big Peter was going with him. "It is an operation and he can help me a lot; up here in the hills it is hard to get anyone."

They had a hearty supper, and after supper, while Little Peter was feeding the cats in the pump room, his father appeared in the doorway. He had on a fur coat and a fur cap, and he looked like a bear. "I'm sorry, old chap," he said. "I may not get back in time to go to the barn."

Little Peter straightened up. "Well, of course if you can't, you can't."

"That's the way to take it. I'll get here if possible."

Little Peter went out and watched his father and Uncle Bob drive away. They were in a high-powered car that had been Big Peter's Christmas present to his brother. "One fee paid for it," he had said when Bob had protested. "I kept a millionaire from going blind."

"Great stuff," said Bob.

"But you don't envy me?"

Bob had shaken his head. "Each man to his own job; I am used to this."

The old dog, Caesar, was curled up under a rug on the back seat as they drove away. He was getting very old, and it was a cold night but he always howled when he was left behind.

After the men were gone, Aunt Jean and Little Peter's mother turned the young people out of the living room and trimmed the tree. And Little Peter and his cousins went into the kitchen to make candy. It was really a most entrancing occupation. On the glowing range was a great saucepan full of molasses and sugar and butter. It boiled and bubbled, and the whole place was soon filled with satisfying fragrance. And there were big white platters with nutmeats on them. And you poured some of the taffy over the nutmeats, and some of it you pulled. And it was while Little Peter and his cousins pulled the taffy that Lucia, tying a pink angel to the top of the tree, looked down at Jean and said, "If you lived in an apartment, what would you do?"

Jean looked up at her and laughed, "I'd move."

"I don't mean that. What would you do about living? I've been watching you and the boys and Bob. You are the center of their world. And I am not the center of mine."

"Well, it is this way," said Jean. "Bob and the boys are so interesting to me that nothing else counts."

"Do you mean that you like it so much?"

"Yes, they are full of the wine of life. When I am with them I seem to drink of it."

Lucia argued, "If you lived in the city you'd have to do as the Romans do."

"There would be a difference, of course," Jean admitted, "but the main thing is to get the right attitude of mind. Bob and the boys are my most gorgeous adventure. And they know it. So they open the gates of their dreams, and off we go together!"

Lucia looked down from the stepladder. "Little Peter has shut the gate of his dreams and locked me out."

"The key is in your own heart, Lucia," Jean said. "When your two Peters become the most important thing in the world to you, you'll become the most important thing to them." Then after a moment, she added, "I always think of my boys as potential leaders of men. I want them to be that. I think they will be."

Lucia came down from the stepladder. "It's Peter's bedtime." She laid her hand on Jean's shoulder. "Do you know that you are a most inspiring person?"

Jean reached up and patted the slender hand. "I know that you are a most beautiful one."

"Oh, beauty," said Lucia, "half of it is my clothes!"

Little Peter went to bed but not to sleep. It was a tell bed with four posts and a blue and white counterpane with a fringe. It had stopped snowing and the open window made a square of blue light. The door that led to his mother's room was a golden space in which he could see her moving back and forth. She had on her warm, thick pussy-cat robe. Peter liked the pussy-cat robe and so did his father. It had white fur at the neck and wrists. He heard his mother open her own window, then she came to the door. "Sleep, Peter?"

"No."

She bent above the bed. "I kissed you once, didn't I? Well, I'll kiss you twice and three times and then you must close your eyes."

She knelt with her arms around him. "And when you wake it will be Christmas morning."

Peter knew that he would wake long before that. He was going out to the barn to see what the animals would do at midnight. If Daddy came, so much the better. But he wasn't going to lose this chance to see whether the cows and the horses and the old sheep who churned the butter, would kneel.

For one moment he was tempted to ask his mother to go with him. But he knew what she would say, "How silly—to think that the animals would." And that would spoil it.

He slept before he knew it and awoke with a start. He wondered if it were midnight, and even while he wondered, he heard the grandfather's clock in the lower hall strike with a jangle of chimes—eleven. He lay, then, waiting until another brief jangle marked the quarter after. He climbed out of bed, gathered up his clothes, and in his bare feet descended the stairs and made his way to the living room. It was all shadowy with the glow of the dim lamp and of the deep-hearted coals. The cats were curled up in a warm heap on the rug. The room was deliciously cozy after the keen air upstairs. He sat on the rug among the little cats and donned his stockings hastily, his shoes and underclothes, his knickers, and jacket. Then he pulled over all his thick sweater, and covered his ears with his knitted cap. He found a pencil and wrote a note that he propped up against the lamp.

"DEAR DADDY: I've gone to the barn. I thought I'd better not wait. I hope you will come. PETER"

He felt very daring as he opened the door and went out into the night. The sky was powdered with stars; it seemed very high and different from the sky in the city which was always blurred with electric lights.

Young Brutus, the watch dog, came out of his kennel, and trotted over the frozen snow ahead of Peter. He made no sound, and in the clear dark he looked long and lean like a wolf. But Little Peter was not afraid of him. He was indeed glad of his company.

The barn was lighted by a single lantern. Back among the shadows were the cows, comfortable on beds of straw. The old butter sheep and a blind mare had open stalls to themselves. Beyond them were the strong work horses and the lighter span, which the doctor drove now and then. Tessie, the barn cat, came down to investigate the invasion. Peter sat on a feed box and took her in his lap and waited. It seemed that there were pigeons up among the rafters and Tessie's kittens in the loft. There was a round barn clock, and it showed a quarter of twelve. Peter felt a tingling sense of excitement. Something must, he felt, in a moment, happen.

And now young Brutus was on his feet—stiff and suspicious— his eyes on the side door by which Peter had entered. The door opened and Peter saw a woman coming in. She wore a long blue cloak and carried a lantern. There was a scarf over her head that hid her face.

Peter knew at once why she had come. She was tired—and there was no room for her at the inn—

He rose to his feet and stood for a moment uncertain, then sent a breathless little cry across the intervening space, "Mary!"

Lucia had awakened to find Peter gone. She had slipped into the pussy-cat robe and sought him downstairs. She had found the note propped up against the lamp. She had dressed hurriedly. The blue cloak and scarf she had borrowed from the hall rack. They belonged to Jean and fell about her own slender figure in voluminous folds.

She had lighted a lantern and made her way to the barn. And now she was saying, her own breath quick, "It is Mother, darling," and Peter with dreams still in his eyes was stammering, "Why, I didn't know you."

"Why did you come, Peter?"

"Well, I thought they might kneel—the animals, you know."

"Oh, at midnight?"

"Yes."

She glanced up at the clock. "Five minutes."

He was anxious. "May I stay?"

"Yes."

"Shall we sit here?" The feed-box was wide enough for both of them. She put her arm around Peter and he leaned against her. The blue cloak enfolded them. The lantern held them close in a circle of its light.

In the moments that followed, the stillness seemed to Lucia to flow up and around them in warm and shining waves. She was aware of all the living things so near in the dark. Shut away from the clamor of the quick and the changing world, she seemed to share something with these dumb and tranquil beasts.

Tranquility! Was it that she had missed? Would Little Peter and Big Peter draw close if she shut them into a world of her own where peace reigned? And could they shut her out if she shut them in?

Little Peter's breathless cry had moved her strangely. He had linked her by his vivid imagination to that serene and gracious presence.

"Mother, it's twelve!" Little Peter's hand clutched her arm. "It's twelve!"

The old clock ticked a round of sixty seconds, another round. Little Peter was on his feet, his eager eyes sweeping the shadows, where dark outlines loomed, unmoving and unchanged.

At last he drew a long, quivering breath. "Oh, they didn't do it, Mother."

She felt she must not fail him. "Darling," she said, "perhaps they knelt—in their hearts."

Far back in his eyes there danced a light—the light which had shone hitherto only for Big Peter. His warm hand went into hers. "Oh, well, it was wonderful to come, wasn't it?"

It was more wonderful than he knew.

And now across the small-paned windows swept the streaming gold of car lights; there was the purr of the engine, then silence. Then the great door slid back and Big Peter peered in. "Who's here?"

Little Peter gave a great shout and fell upon him. "It's Mother, Daddy, and me."

"Lucia?"

She came forward. "Yes, where's Bob?"

"He stayed all night." Big Peter's voice trailed away. He stood staring. Lucia in that blue cloak among the golden shadows. Why, the thing was like an old painting! "Do you know," he asked, "that you make me think of the Madonna?"

"Little Peter saw it too," she said. She laid her hand on his arm, looking up at him. "When I came in he called me . . . Mary."

He was at once aware that she was deeply moved. His own heartbeats quickened. His arms went around her. "All mothers are Marys, my darling." She leaned her head against him, loving his tenderness. She put her arm around Little Peter and he leaned against her. The blue cloak enfolded them. With the child they stood in the circle of light made by the lantern.

And it was Christmas morning!

Joey's Miracle

Hartley F. Dailey

"Miracles just don't happen anymore." But 6-year-old Joey didn't believe that for a minute—he was sure God would bring him a bicycle. With the Depression raising fiscal havoc and most people struggling just to find food for the table, clearly the little boy was setting himself up for certain disillusionment.

(Hartley Dailey, author of "The Red Mittens," Christmas in My Heart, 1, *and "Yet Not One of Them Shall Fall,"* Christmas in My Heart, 3, *has become one of the series' most appreciated living authors. This third story of his is just as special.*

They say the age of miracles is past. They say the prophets are all dead, that shining angels no longer fly down from the realm above, bringing divine messages to mortal men, handing out rewards to the good and punishment to the guilty. All of which is true, of course. One seldom meets a prophet these days, and angels are a remarkably scarce commodity, even in storybooks.

But neither prophets nor angels are absolutely essential to a miracle. Rewards—or punishment—may come at the hands of the most unlikely individuals, and the most mundane of gifts may waken wonder in the eyes of a small boy. Let me tell you the story of Joey's bicycle.

It happened in the depths of the great Depression of the thirties. I had come up from the hills to find a good steady job in the city. There I meet Betty, and we fell in love and were married. Soon we bought a nice house in a good neighborhood and settled down for life, or so we thought. But you know the saying about the best-laid plans of mice and men. Came the Depression and I lost my job. We were faced with house payments, a family to feed and clothe, and very little money in the bank. Like many others, I could see very little hope of any better times in the near future.

Now it so happened I had a little farm back in the hills, which I had inherited from my grandfather. Many times, throughout the years, friends had urged me to sell it, to invest the money, or use it to help pay for my city place. But I had stubbornly held on to it, partly because it made a nice vacation retreat, and partly because I loved the old place, the first home I had ever known.

So at this juncture, faced with the prospect of losing everything we owned, we decided to cut our losses and get out while we still had something left. We sold our home for just enough to pay off the mortgage, a sizeable loss, but we were fortunate to get off so lightly. At least we still had a home back in the hills, not much it is true, but free and clear of any encumbrance. We had 40 acres on which to raise our food, at least. We were better off than thousands of others. So on a clear spring morning we set off, with all our possessions following in a truck, to make our home in a little cabin in the hills.

Throughout the months, because of doctor's bills,

41

taxes, and other unavoidable expenses, our savings slowly dwindled. I had bought a couple of cows, some chickens, and some pigs, and we managed to raise enough food for our own use, plus a little to sell. But of course, prices were very low, and after all, how much can one raise on 40 hilly acres?

We were facing our second Christmas on the farm, and prospects were very poor. Our older children, David, 12, and Melissa, 10, were old enough to understand our poverty. They could accept the fact of having only an extra-good dinner, plus maybe some warm socks or mittens, for Christmas. But Joey was 6, and Joey wanted a bicycle. Useless to explain to him that bicycles cost a lot of money, and only rich little boys could have such luxuries. He was firmly convinced Santa Claus would bring him one. No use, either, to tell him Santa Claus didn't come to see poor little boys. Santa Claus had been to see him before, and he didn't understand the difference. With the help of his sister, he wrote a letter to the old saint, and gave it to me to mail.

Some time later, his friends at school must have cast some doubt on the power, or maybe even the existence, of Santa Claus. Or perhaps he simply decided to take his problem to a higher power. At any rate, he came to me one evening as I read the paper, after the chores were done.

"I'm sure I'll get my bicycle now, Dad," he said.

"Why is that?" I asked absently.

"'Cause Johnny said, if you pray to God, you're sure to get your wish." Johnny was his best school friend. "And that's just what I'm gonna' do," he concluded.

"Oh, Joey, Joey"—I took him in my arms —"don't

you know God can't grant every wish we make? What if there's some other little boy, one who needs a bike much worse than you do? Wouldn't God have to grant his wish instead?"

He wasn't convinced. "I don't know about needs," he said confidently, "but I'm sure God could never find a boy who *wants* one more."

So things stood on Saturday, just a week before Christmas. Joey still included a plea for his bicycle every time he said his prayers. And he went around with such a cheerful smile, as though the coveted property were already on the back porch. He was so good it was almost insufferable.

We had saved up a whole crate of eggs, which I intended to sell in the city, as well as a considerable quantity of turnips, a few apples, and a few potatoes we thought we could spare. On that Saturday morning I set out for the city, determined to sell my produce to the greatest advantage and get what little Christmas I could for everyone. Joey had wanted to go along, but I wouldn't permit it, for the weather was bitter cold, and it was a long trip. Besides, I expected to spend a lot of time walking the streets. It would be too much for a 6-year-old. Later, I was glad I hadn't brought him.

It was about three o'clock in the afternoon when I had finally sold my produce, and such shopping as I could afford was done. I had parked my car and walked over much of the business section, since I had a trailer and couldn't park it easily. I was cold, bone weary, and my feet were soaking wet from walking in the snow. Because of this, I took a shortcut through the alley, past the police station. Thus it was that I came upon the auction.

The police department employees, as they do periodically, were auctioning off an accumulation of unclaimed articles. Already, when I came on the scene, they had sold a surprising miscellany of lost, abandoned, or confiscated items: two old cars, guns, bicycles, luggage, clothing, even one sad-looking, half-frozen hound dog.

The last item of the day was on the block, a little boy's 16-inch bicycle. It was a sad little wreck—its paint all gone, its fenders bent, one tire flat, and the handlebars drooping. Still, with a little paint, a little hammer and wrench work, and with that tire patched, how different it would look! Trouble was, after such little Christmas shopping as I had done, and buying enough gasoline to get me back home, I had only a single half dollar in my pocket.

The auctioneer, a big paunchy, red-faced police sergeant, was calling desperately for bids. In vain he called for $5, $2—$1. Nobody seemed interested. Finally, just as he seemed on the point of losing his voice completely, he stopped shouting, looked over the crowd in a kind of exasperated way, then said in a voice half pleading, half threatening, "Please, for Heaven's sake, won't somebody give me a bid, just *any* bid—but get it started."

That half dollar burned like a red hot coal in my pocket. Should I try it? It was ridiculous, of course. Start it that low, and somebody was sure to top my bid. And I didn't have any more money, not a single penny, to bid any higher. But I had to do it.

"Fifty cents," I called out.

"Bang," went the gavel.

"Mister," said the old sergeant, "you've bought a bicycle."

I've had a soft place in my heart for big red-faced policemen ever since.

Some fellow in the crowd started to protest, saying he hadn't been given a chance to bid before it sold. He didn't like such high-handed tactics, and he was making no bones about it. The sergeant turned on him with a baleful scowl. "True," he stormed, "you wasn't. And where was you, may I ask, when I was standin' here screamin' myself hoarse, just to get an openin' bid? It's cold in this here shed, an' I been standin' here all afternoon, just tryin' to coax another nickel out of you tightwads. It's near my quittin' time, an' I got a lot of work to do yet, writin' up the records of these sales. I'm quittin' here an' now. This gentleman bought the bike, an' there's an end to it!"

I took my purchase away, loaded it in my trailer, and covered it with the sacks in which I had hauled my turnips to town. Christmas day, its tire patched, its fenders and handlebars straightened, and with a bright new coat of paint, it stood beneath our Christmas tree. And if that old sergeant could have seen the joy on the face of one little boy, I'm sure he would have been glad for all the cold and hoarseness he suffered on account of it.

Joey took it all very much for granted. "See, Daddy," he told me very confidently. "God didn't find another little boy who needed a bike more than me. Or at least not one who *wanted* it more," he added.

That bicycle proved to be of much better stuff than its first appearance indicated. Joey rode it up hill and down dale, till he had quite outgrown it. In fact, you can still see it hanging from a couple of pegs on my garage wall, and it still looks better than it did the day I bought it.

Of course, Joey is a grown man now, with a little Joey of his own. More than six feet two, he is a big strapping fellow who did his stint in the Marines during the Korean war and came home to fill a much better job than his daddy ever had. A hardheaded, intensely practical individual, you would say, with no nonsense about him. But if ever you should meet him, don't tell him the age of miracles is past. He'd never believe you.

Christmas in the New World

Rosina Kiehlbauch

The year was 1874 and the Dakota prairies were lonely, cold, and virtually treeless. How was a German immigrant family, transplanted from the steppes of Russia only three months before, supposed to find a Christmas where not even a Lutheran church had been constructed?

Where would a tree come from? Where, for that matter, would toys, gifts? This was the dilemma that faced Johannes and Codray (Katherina), but they set about making the best of it.

Unique in Christmas literature is Rosina Kiehlbach's trilogy of three Christmases (1874, 1884, 1894) on the Dakota frontier. Nothing I have ever read is comparable to these three accounts: not only do they have power and pathos, but they also graphically reveal the interweaving changes in frontier life.

Rosina Kiehlbach's daughter, Catherine Sherry, felt so strongly that these memories deserved a wider audience that she made them available to the editors of The American Historical Society of Germans from Russia in Lincoln, Nebraska, who ran them in three issues of their Journal.

For further information on the Kristkindle and Pelznickel, see "A Pennsylvania Deutsch Christmas." We begin with the earliest of the three accounts.

Eighteen hundred and seventy-four. In a sod house on the Dakota prairie, 6,000 miles from last Christmas in Russia, Johannes and Codray Kulbach were facing the holiday season with many misgivings.

Since September, when they took up their Clear Lake homestead, these south Russian German immigrants had been so busy putting up a sod house in which to live and sod shelters for their farm animals and plowing fields that the trip to Yankton for holiday supplies and a few extra comforts for the long winter had been repeatedly postponed.

What would they do about Christmas for their three little children? The demands of homesteading left no time for the pioneer parents to provide more than the bare necessities for pioneer life. There was still money in the black lacquer cash box. It had provided first class passage on the S.S. *Brunswick* from the old country. In the new country they had bought farm implements, a team of horses, and the necessary household furnishings. It wasn't the lack of money; it was the lack of time now that snow had come so early and the menace of a Dakota blizzard that made the two-day trip to town hazardous even with good horses.

During the weeks spent on the seemingly barren prairie, the immigrants had learned to solve all kinds of problems. Surely somehow they would also solve the problem of a tree and gifts for the children's first

45

Christmas in the land of their adoption. Was it not for the children's sake that they had left their comfortable home in south Russia and come to America? They must not fail in this their first Christmas celebration.

Johannes and his wife were courageous pioneers, descendants of liberty-loving Swabians, who almost a century earlier, rather than submit to compulsory military service in Württemberg, had immigrated to the wild steppes of south Russia and there, under the direct protection of the Russian Crown, had built their homes, tilled the soil, and kept the holy days of the Lutheran Church with appropriate celebrations. Surely God was a God of the prairies as well as of the steppes, and if He marked the sparrow's fall He would also mark the little soddie so trustfully launched on the prairie's endless sea of grass.

In the land of the Dakotas there was no cathedral with its familiar Advent services to remind old and young that the holidays were drawing near. The Church Almanac in which the homesteaders checked each day (there was no other way of keeping track of the days) showed that the Trinitatis Sundays would soon change to the Advent Sundays. In the old country this was the time for the housewife to think of holiday preparations such as baking *Lebkuchen*, *Springerlei*, and other Christmas goodies that improved with age.

In 1874 there were no near, neighborly housewives who were also making Christmas plans and with whom one could exchange ideas; no shops to visit; no evergreens to conjure up pictures of holiday splendor; and nothing in the soddie with which to make fitting gifts.

Fortunately the children were still so engrossed with their "bon voyage" presents that in spite of the snow, Christmas was not holding the usual importance in their childish thoughts and play. But when they helped their mother set up the Christmas twigs, the two little sisters were reminded of similar preparations for the holidays in Russia and asked, "Will Christmas come on the prairie so far from Russia and Grandfather and Grandmother?"

It was more because of habit than of faith in what she did, that Codray had cut willows and arranged them in a crock on the kitchen window near the adobe stove. In fruitful south Russia, she, like her mother before her, had always cut peach or cherry twigs and by soaking them in warm water had forced them to blossom for the coming of the Christ Child. On the Dakota prairie there were no fruit trees for Christmas bloom—only here and there a few willows by a shallow lake or slow-flowing creek. In this new country what outward signs for Christmas could they substitute for the dear, familiar symbols of old country Christmas celebration?

It was clear to these pioneer parents that a prairie Christmas could not be an elaborate celebration like in Russia, but they were sure it could be a Christmas celebration nevertheless. They assured the children that the Christ Child would come to good children no matter where they lived. Content that Christmas would come because Father and Mother had said so, the two sisters began to wonder what *Kristkindle* and *Pelznickel* would bring them if they were diligent and learned the lessons and did the tasks that Father and Mother set for them. From their superior knowledge of four and six Christmases they tried to impress upon their 2-year-old brother all the joys of the holiday season.

The children were delighted with the blooming of the Christmas twigs. To them it was one more assurance that *Kristkindle* was coming. What if, instead of flowers, the willows had produced soft, fuzzy buds that looked very much like fur-wrapped Indian babies clinging to their mothers' backs? These little "papoose willows" became a pre-holiday source of much pleasure and excitement.

The problem of how to get a suitable Christmas tree was still unsolved, but Codray's attempt to foster the Christmas spirit in America with willows so heartened the family that Johannes thought he'd try his hand with the pliable osiers. But how could one make a beautiful Christmas tree out of a straight, uninspiring willow? "Graceful as a willow wand" might serve the poet, but how could it serve the pioneers whose children expected that tree of all trees, a Christmas tree with many heavily laden branches?

Johannes put on his Russian *Pelz* and tall fur cap and went down to the lakeshore. There he selected a straight, stout willow about the thickness of his thumb and hoped for inspiration. He took it to his workbench, bored holes into it about where branches could be and whittled down willow tips to fit the holes. In spite of the make-believe branches, it was only a bare, stiff, ungainly tree skeleton, but somehow there was an innate, sturdy courage about it, and who could say that the Christmas spirit was not in its heart?

Codray was completely surprised when her husband showed her what he had done out at the workbench. "Can we make a willow blossom like a Christmas tree?" he paraphrased apologetically.

For a moment his wife was really dismayed by the unchristmas-like tree. But its meek, comical, scarecrow appearance touched her heart, and its utter forlornness aroused her maternal instinct. She wanted something with which to cover its nakedness. "Of course we can make it blossom like a Christmas tree," she said, talking to keep up her courage until she could think of something to do. "We haven't the abundance of Russia, but hasn't God blessed all our efforts? Didn't we take what the prairie had to offer and make a warm sod house? Buffalo chips and prairie grass have furnished fuel, wild fowls and fish have been our food. Surely a Christmas tree is not impossible when the spirit of Christmas is abroad. Just come with me and we will make it blossom." And she led the way back to the house.

In the soddie the homesteaders collected every scrap of plain paper they could find. Even the margins of the few treasured copies of the pioneer newspaper, the *Dakota Freie Presse*, were sacrificed. Codray went to the homemade cupboard and unwrapped her winter's supply of Frank's chicory. Many settlers used chicory as a coffee substitute. She soaked the brilliant red wrapper in water to extract the color. Into the red dye-bath she dipped the scraps of paper. When they were dry she cut the colored pieces into fringe and carefully, lovingly twisted them around each stiff, make-believe willow branch. All left-over scraps were fashioned into rosettes for ornamenting the tips of the branches. Such a Christmas tree as was "never seen on land or sea" began to blossom in the prairie soddie. The tree was its own inspiration for presents. A willow with a twisted root was fashioned into a hobby horse for little brother. But it looked so lonesome that Johannes made hobby horses for each of the girls also. Willow whistles and tops suggested themselves.

Since Christmas and dolls are almost synonymous in the minds of little girls, dolls would have to be produced somehow. Dolls? Codray thought of cookie dolls. They would be novelties. But a novelty is usually short-lived, and among children with good teeth and healthy appetites, edible novelties would not last long. Then, though their tummies might feel full, their hearts would be empty after Christmas day. Codray would have to devise more substantial dolls. Would the Christmas tree give the inspiration?

After the children were asleep in their trundle bed, the parents brought the tree into the house and worked on their Christmas preparations. Their little willow emblem of Christmas stood up courageously and tried its best to fill the exalted position for which it was destined. Surely they could not fail the tree or the children who placed such confidence in them. They had used willows for fuel, for fishpoles, for rabbit snares, for brooms, for baskets, and now for a Christmas tree. Why not willow dolls in keeping with their prairie Christmas motif?

The young mother took a bunch of slender willow-tips and tied them together for the body of the doll. Her skillful fingers fashioned a cloth-covered head and her husband whittled the arms. When dressed, "Willowminna Americana" was very intriguing indeed. To keep "Willowminna" from being lonesome, Codray started to make a whole family of willow dolls and a Russian "Ami" to help care for them. She clapped her hands with delight when her husband evened the tips of the willows and stood the dolls in a row on the drop-

leaf table. The little girls surely would enjoy dolls that could stand.

As the homesteaders surveyed the row of dolls, they noticed that the oil in the glass lamp was getting low. They knew there would be no chance to replenish the one gallon of kerosene oil before spring. But this was Christmas. It would take another evening or two to complete the doll family and the willow trundle bed that Johannes had suggested. So the happy parents decided to work on and forget for the time being all the difficulties of pioneering. After the holidays they could conserve kerosene and use only the wild goose lamp, the prairie substitute for the whale oil lamp of New England's pioneer days.

The wild goose lamp—a wick soaked in melted goose fat—was a greasy, sputtering, sooty affair at its best, but it gave sufficient light during the short evenings that the homesteaders allowed themselves for basket weaving, harness oiling, plowshare polishing, wool carding, and such other pioneer occupations that depended as much on touch as on sight.

On the last evening of their Christmas preparations, Codray sat close to the brightly polished glass lamp and sewed up the little doll feather ticks and pillow cases that she and her husband had filled with wild goose feathers. Then from the tin foil that had been carefully saved from Johannes' tobacco, they shaped two little cups and two little saucers for a tea set, and covered a few nuts with the remaining tin foil.

Fervently Johannes wished there were more nuts and candies. But in October, when on one of the infrequent trips to Yankton, the storekeeper had suggested to the immigrant that it might be well to make some purchases for Christmas, Johannes could not take it seriously. Who can get into the Christmas spirit when days are warm and the sun is shining brightly? But because the storekeeper suggested it, Johannes made a few desultory purchases. He felt awkward about it, for he and his wife had always gone to Odessa together for Christmas shopping. Now alone he did not know just what to buy. Of course, candy and nuts were essential to Christmas cheer so he bought some, thinking to get more when his wife would be with him on the next trip. But the early snows had prevented any more trips to Yankton. So, the few tin foil nuts and the red rosettes made from the paper scraps would have to make as grand a showing as possible on the Christmas tree. There would be no candles. Wild goose candles were out of the question, and there was no tallow.

Although it was late when finally the few nuts had been fastened on the tree, the rosettes adjusted, and the tree returned to the workbench, yet Codray took time to set the sponge for the day-before-Christmas baking and Johannes laid the fire in the adobe stove, before they retired.

The next morning, after a breakfast of milk and "Gritz," Bevela and Katya, quivering with excitement, did the dishes to the tunes of "O du fröhliche" and "Von Himmel hoch" while their mother tended to the bread sponge. The singing was interrupted with many giggles and squeals of delight. For every time the dough gave a squeak as their mother worked it down, the girls had to join in and exclaim over how light and fine the Christmas goodies were going to be.

The white flour was very low in the barrel, but since it was Christmas and there was so little with which to celebrate, Codray trusted that the good Father in heaven would stretch the flour as He had the widow's supply of meal, and let them celebrate with extra goodies for the children and for the stranger who might come their way. What fun the two little sisters had putting raisin eyes on the dolls and animals and doves of peace that their mother made from dough. For the gifts that Codray desired to give and could not, she baked a dough replica and gave it in edible form.

In the middle of the afternoon, when the little sisters felt they could no longer be on their best behavior, there was a loud knocking on the door and *Pelznickel* with book and switch came in. He questioned the little girls about their conduct and examined them in their ABC's, asked what church hymns they could sing, whether they were learning to read and write and had started the shorter catechism. Having received favorable answers and impressions, *Pelznickel* gave each a few candies and nuts and a dove of peace carrying a little willow twig in its mouth. Since they were such good, studious children, he assured them, *"Kristkindle* will remember you on the morrow."

Kristkindle came while the children slept.

On Christmas morning the little willow Christmas tree had a surprising array of gifts. Some looked so good that the children not only wanted to, but could eat them. Everyone had been remembered. Even the dog, Watch, had not been forgotten. When the children took him his cake of bran, it looked so appetizing that they shared it with him.

What a blessed Christmas morning! Cold and sparkling outside. Everything transformed with white shining brightness. The dry grass that had given the soddie a wild, shaggy look now made it look like a white loaf cake covered with coconut frosting. A few, large snowflakes lazily zig-zagged outside the window. The children thought they moved slowly to get a glimpse of the Christmas cheer in the soddie.

The children were delighted with their prairie Christmas tree. No one had ever seen such a tree. Nor such dolls! Dolls that could stand! Three hobby horses went a-prancing! Father taught the children how to spin the tops and blow the whistles. Mother gave each a tiny willow basket of nuts, candy, and cookies. Nowhere in all "Kristkindledom" were there three happier children than in the soddie on the Clear Lake homestead.

By eleven o'clock the Christmas wild goose was roasting merrily in the adobe oven. Toys were laid aside. Since they could not go to the usual eleven o'clock Christmas morning church service, the family gathered around, and Father read the Christmas story, and together they sang the Christmas songs.

What a Christmas celebration! New world willow dolls, willow doll beds, willow whistles, willow tops, willow hobby horses, willow baskets, and a willow tree—a new world willow Christmas symphony, but the old world Christmas story and the old world Christmas songs.

And so it was "on Christmas day in the morning" out on the Dakota prairie in 1874.

Charlie's Blanket

Wendy Miller

It was a bitterly cold Canadian Christmas. Cold in more ways than one. Mary could see precious little to be thankful for, deserted as they had been by husband and father. Everywhere else but in their dreary little flat, Christmas took the cold away. Worst of all, the deadly acid of bitterness was gradually destroying the forsaken little family.

All but Becky, who was content with but a worn-out rag of a blanket—and Charlie.

Some months ago, as I opened my mail, I noticed a packet from Canada. Wendy Miller, a homemaker from Alberta, in her letter, said this about the story she enclosed: "This story really happened. Very few facts are changed at all. I did change our names, because I did not wish our family to be easily recognized. I know it's true, because I lived it, and Becky is my sister. I realize that the story is not very polished and maybe not even very good. I am not a writer. I do write a lot of stories and poetry, but only for my family; this is the first story I have ever shared with anyone else. The words just kind of went from heart to paper."

Mrs. Miller was modest. The text that follows needed very little editing. And the story . . . well, I guess the fact that it leapfrogged over all those other stories by well-known authors will tell you how it affected me.

Mary hurried to get her children fed and dressed. It was a cold December day, and they had a long way to walk. Mary cleaned houses five days a week; it was the only work she could find that would allow her to also take care of her three small girls at the same time. She would drop the older two off at the elementary school and take 3-year-old Becky with her. The girls came to her for lunch, and she would be back home again before they were home from school in the afternoon. It was a good arrangement, and it kept her off welfare. She wanted help from no one.

"Becky," she called, "hurry; we're all ready to go!"

Becky ran to the door, a ragged doll with all its hair loved off cradled in her arms. "I'm all ready, Mama, but we forgot to dress Charlie."

Mary glanced at the clock and back down at her daughter's smiling face. Quickly she dressed the doll, wrapped it in its blanket, and handed it back to Becky. Then the little family went out into the cold, dark early morning.

"Mama,"—Laura, 7, and the oldest, took Mary's hand—"I'm sorry I forgot Charlie. Are we awfully late?"

"No, Laura, we're not awfully late."

"I don't know why we have to dress that stupid doll of hers anyway," complained Cindy. Since she was 6 and in the first grade, she thought of herself as all grown up—and to her, Charlie was a big waste of time.

Two years ago Mary might have agreed with her. They had been well off then and wanted for nothing. Mary's thoughts traveled back to other times and compared then to now as she had done a million times. One day everything was fine, and the next day her husband was gone. All he had left behind was a note to say goodbye. No, he had also left behind a wife, three small girls, and an empty bank account.

As soon as the shock had worn off, Mary tried to start a new life, but it was so hard. She had never had to work outside the home before. Now she was cleaning houses to keep the girls fed. Their clothes were handed down from her employers' children. Most of all she regretted having to make them walk so far every day, especially in the cold.

As for the radical change in lifestyle, the girls had just accepted it as part of life. Laura and Cindy helped as much as they could and tried not to complain. Becky found happiness in her doll. Charlie was her whole world. She never quit smiling as long as she had Charlie. He was always to be dressed for the weather and then wrapped in the precious blanket. It was just an old scrap of a blanket that somebody must have dropped in the parking lot; Becky found it there, Mary washed it, and now it was Charlie's. Was Charlie a waste of time? No, Mary decided; he was Becky's happiness, and that most certainly was not a waste of time.

As they neared the school, the girls hugged Mary as they always did day after day, then ran in. Farther down the street, Mary turned in at the Littles'—Monday's house. The Littles had been getting ready for Christmas, it seemed, because there was a wreath on the door with a big red bow. Mary was prepared to see all the fancy trimmings inside. Becky wasn't.

"Ooh, Charlie," she whispered as if afraid that her voice might disturb the splendor, "look at what Mrs. Little got." The room was gaily decorated for Christmas, and in the corner stood a huge Christmas tree. The silver star shining on the top almost touched the ceiling. Glass ornaments, garlands, and tinsel were tastefully arranged on the branches, and underneath was a mountain of parcels wrapped with ribbons and bows.

Mary took Becky's coat and hung it up. The little girl just stood looking at the tree. "Becky, I have to get to work now. Promise you won't touch anything."

"I promise, Mama." And she crawled into a big easy chair, and there she stayed for the entire morning, pointing out the pretty ornaments to Charlie and guessing what might be in each of the packages.

Laura and Cindy came in at lunch, but they hardly looked at the tree. It hurt to look at it. They knew that there would be no tree for them—just like last year. Money was not to be spent on anything they could do without. They knew it—but it still hurt.

The day replayed itself on Tuesday at the Johnsons', on Wednesday at the Harrises', Thursday at the Krebbs', and Friday at the Fishers'. But on Saturday they were home.

After spending a week in the various houses all decked in glorious holiday fashion, Becky suddenly seemed to realize that she was missing out on something. "Why does everyone have a tree in the house, Mama? Why are there so many presents? Is it somebody's birthday? Why don't we have a tree?"

Mary had known the question would be asked. Laura and Cindy looked up from the floor where they were playing, waiting for her answer. Mary put away her mending and pulled Becky up onto her lap. "You're a very smart girl. It *is* somebody's birthday, and I'll tell you all about Him. His name is Jesus, and He was born Christmas Day." And Mary told the girls how it came to happen and why there is a Christmas.

Becky hugged Charlie close. "Ooh, the poor Baby. Was it very cold in the stable? I wouldn't want to sleep in a stable, would you? I wish I could go there and see it, though."

"We *can* see it," Mary said, and she put her daughter off her knee. "Girls, get your coats on. We're going for a walk."

Down the street was a church. Every Christmas a large crèche was set up. There was a wooden stable full of straw and large ceramic figures. High above hung a star. The girls were awed by the simple but beautiful scene. It was just as Mary had said it was from the story in the Bible. Becky didn't want to leave even when the cold seeped through her clothing and made her shiver.

The next week was just as hard for them. Everywhere they went, it seemed that the world was taunting them with a Christmas that wasn't to be theirs. In the malls carols played, and parents loaded up with the latest toys and games. As Mary picked out economy packs of socks and underwear for the girls' gifts she tried not to look in the other carts. At Safeway she whipped through the express line with one lone pack of spaghetti for their Christmas dinner. She laughed at the long line-ups of people with their carts full of turkey and fixings. But the laugh was hollow, because she would have loved to be one of those standing in line. Outside, families shouted and laughed as they picked out what each considered the perfect tree and then strapped it to the roof of their car. Mary tried not to notice. It was Laura and Cindy that finally made her heart well over with bitterness.

Somehow, when you are an adult, you can take whatever is dished out. You take things in stride and make the best of a situation. But, oh how different it is when your child is hurting! Nothing hurts a mother more than the sorrow of her child. And that's how it was with Mary. The school was focused on Christmas, which was only to be expected in December. The teachers had the children making ornaments and stringing popcorn for their trees at home. They wrote letters to Santa. At recess, the children told of the gifts they were expecting. Laura and Cindy said nothing. They did as they were expected in class and tried to avoid the other children at recess. It was at home that they expressed their hurt and anger at the world for leaving them out of Christmas. So the bitterness grew in Mary from the heartache of her girls.

Every carol and decoration seemed to make her colder. Every Christmas card or call of "Merry Christmas" made her hate the season more. Laura and Cindy, taking the cue from their mother as children often do, developed the same attitude. Only little Becky was immune. She rocked Charlie in her arms and told him again and again about Baby Jesus, who was born in a stable. She begged the girls daily to take her to the church so she could see the story "for true." They would take her grudgingly and drag her back home long before she was finished looking.

Christmas morning came in a flurry of snow. Laura and Cindy woke up cold. They ran into Mary's room and burrowed under the covers with her to warm up. Mary cuddled them close and kissed their foreheads.

"Merry Christmas," she said.

"Merry Christmas, Mama," they echoed.

"I'm afraid there aren't a lot of gifts for you girls, but you go wake up Becky, and you can open what there is," she said resignedly.

The girls jumped out of the bed and ran to get their sister while Mary got up and dressed. Too soon, they were back.

"Where *is* she, Mama? We can't find her!" The words hit Mary like a truck. The three raced through the house calling her name, checking every closet and corner. They checked the yard and the neighbor's yard. No Becky! They must have missed her when they checked the house, Mary thought. She never goes off alone. They searched the house again.

"Dear Lord, please help me find her," she prayed as she rechecked every spot a child could possibly be in. "I'm sorry for my selfishness. The gifts and the dinner that I prayed for are not important. Forget them and just give me back my Becky." She was frantic now.

Then she noticed Charlie. He was carefully positioned in a chair facing a window. Mary's heart raced with her thoughts. Charlie was *never* out of Becky's sight. And where was his blanket? Becky always insisted that his blanket be wrapped tightly around him at all times. Suddenly she *knew!*

"Stay here!" she admonished the girls as she flew out the door into the dark and snowy morning. Down the street she ran, until she could see the church. Then she slowed, and tears of release ran down her face as she caught sight of her daughter. The star from the crèche was shining down on the manger where Becky had climbed in and was busily covering the Baby Jesus with the ratty scrap of a blanket. As she neared, Mary could hear Becky talking:

"You must be cold. I knew the snow would be falling on You. This is Charlie's blanket, but we will give it to You. He has me to keep him warm." She looked up when she heard the footsteps. "Oh! Hi, Mama." Becky smiled her beautiful innocent smile. "I was afraid He might have thought we forgot about Him on His birthday."

Mary plucked her out of the straw and held her tight, the tears now raining unchecked. "I *did* forget, Honey. . . . Dear Lord, I'm sorry I forgot." Then she tenderly carried her daughter home, filled at last with Christmas joy.

With Christmas carols to cheer them on, they hung the popcorn strings and ornaments on Mary's tallest houseplant. A star made of tin foil perched on the top. They put the presents underneath, and there was just enough to fit nicely under the little tree. And best of all, Mary made a birthday cake. With their hands joined around the table, they all sang "Happy Birthday, Dear Jesus, happy birthday to You. . . ."

As for Charlie, cradled tightly in Becky's arms—even without his blanket, he was warm.

A Day of Pleasant Bread

David Grayson

When Christmas nears, our thoughts often turn to those less fortunate than we—the poor, the needy, the destitute. But what if there are none in that condition nearby? If so, would one then—perish the thought!—have to resort to inviting the rich?

(Pulitzer Prize winning author Ray Stannard Baker [1870-1946] led a double life. In public he was the renowned editor, journalist, and author of the monumental eight-volume life of Woodrow Wilson. In private, under the pen name of David Grayson, he was free to roam the country as a home-spun philosopher and humorist. In the process, we are all the richer for such books as Adventures in Contentment, Adventures in Friendship, The Friendly Road, Great Possessions, *and* Adventures in Understanding.*)*

They have all gone now, and the house is very still. For the first time this evening I can hear the familiar sound of the December wind blustering about the house, complaining at closed doorways, asking questions at the shutters; but here in my room, under the green reading lamp, it is warm and still. Although Harriet has closed the doors, covered the coals in the fireplace, and said goodnight, the atmosphere still seems to tingle with the electricity of genial humanity.

The parting voice of the Scotch preacher still booms in my ears:

"This," said he, as he was going out of our door, wrapped like an Arctic highlander in cloaks and tippets, "has been a day of pleasant bread."

One of the very pleasantest I can remember!

I sometimes think we expect too much of Christmas Day. We try to crowd into it the long arrears of kindliness and humanity of the whole year. As for me, I like to take my Christmas a little at a time, all through the year. And thus I drift along into the holidays—let them overtake me unexpectedly—waking up some fine morning and suddenly saying to myself:

"Why, this is Christmas Day!"

How the discovery makes one bound out of his bed! What a new sense of life and adventure it imparts! Almost anything may happen on a day like this—one thinks. I may meet friends I have not seen before in years. Who knows? I may discover that this is a far better and kindlier world than I had ever dreamed it could be.

So I sing out to Harriet as I go down:

"Merry Christmas, Harriet"—and not waiting for her sleepy reply, I go down and build the biggest, warmest, friendliest fire of the year. Then I get into my thick coat and mittens and open the back door. All around the sill, deep on the step, and all about the yard lies the drifted snow: it has transformed my wood pile into a grotesque Indian mound, and it frosts the roof of my barn like a wedding cake. I go at it lustily with my wooden shovel, clearing out a pathway to the gate. . . .

All the morning as I went about my chores I had a peculiar sense of expected pleasure. It seemed certain to me that something unusual and adventurous was about to happen—and if it did not happen offhand, why, I was there to make it happen! When I went in to breakfast (do you know the fragrance of broiling bacon when you have worked for an hour before breakfast on a morning of zero weather? If you do not, consider that heaven still has gifts in store for you!)—when I went in to breakfast, I fancied that Harriet looked preoccupied, but I was too busy just then (hot corn muffins) to make an inquiry, and I knew by experience that the best solvent of secrecy is patience.

"David," said Harriet presently, "the cousins can't come!"

"Can't come!" I exclaimed.

"Why, you act as if you were delighted."

"No—well, yes," I said. "I knew that some extraordinary adventure was about to happen!"

"Adventure! It's a cruel disappointment—I was all ready for them."

"Harriet," I said, "adventure is just what we make it. And aren't we to have the Scotch preacher and his wife?"

"But I've got such a *good* dinner."

"Well," I said, "there are no two ways about it: it must be eaten! You may depend upon me to do my duty."

"We'll have to send out into the highways and compel them to come in," said Harriet ruefully.

I had several choice observations I should have liked to make upon this problem, but Harriet was plainly not listening; she sat with her eyes fixed reflectively on the coffeepot. I watched her for a moment, then I remarked:

"There aren't any."

"David," she exclaimed, "how did you know what I was thinking about?"

"I merely wanted to show you," I said, "that my genius is not properly appreciated in my own household. You thought of highways, didn't you? Then you thought of the poor; especially the poor on Christmas Day; then of Mrs. Heney, who isn't poor anymore, having married John Daniels; and then I said 'There aren't any.'"

Harriet laughed.

"It has come to a pretty pass," she said, "when there are no poor people to invite to dinner on Christmas Day."

"It's a tragedy, I'll admit," I said, "but let's be logical about it."

"I am willing," said Harriet, "to be as logical as you like."

"Then," I said, "having no poor to invite to dinner, we must necessarily try the rich. That's logical, isn't it?"

"Who?" asked Harriet, which is just like a woman. Whenever you get a good healthy argument started with her, she will suddenly short-circuit it, and want to know if you mean Mr. Smith, or Joe Perkins's boys, which I maintain is *not* logical.

"Well, there are the Starkweathers," I said.

"David!"

"They're rich, aren't they?"

"Yes, but you know how they live—what dinners they have— and besides, they probably have a houseful of company."

"Weren't you telling me the other day how many people who were really suffering were too proud to let anyone know about it? Weren't you advising the necessity of getting acquainted with people and finding out—tactfully, of course—you made a point of fact—what the trouble was?"

"But I was talking of *poor* people."

"Why shouldn't a rule that is good for poor people be equally as good for rich people? Aren't they proud?"

"Oh, you can argue," observed Harriet.

"And I can act, too," I said. "I am now going over to invite the Starkweathers. I heard a rumor that their cook has left them, and I expect to find them starving in their parlor. Of course they'll be very haughty and proud, but I'll be tactful, and when I go away I'll casually leave a diamond tiara in the front hall."

"What *is* the matter with you this morning?"

"Christmas," I said.

I can't tell how pleased I was with the enterprise I had in mind: it suggested all sort of amusing and surprising developments. Moreover, I left Harriet, finally, in the breeziest of spirits, having quite forgotten her disappointment over the nonarrival of the cousins.

"If you *should* get the Starkweathers—"

"'In the bright lexicon of youth,'" I observed, "'there is no such word as fail.'"

So I set off up the town road. A team or two had already been that way and had broken a track through the snow. The sun was now fully up, but the air still tingled with the electricity of zero weather. And the fields! I have seen the fields of June and the fields of October,

but I think I never saw our countryside, hills and valleys, tree spaces and brook bottoms, more enchantingly beautiful than it was this morning. Snow everywhere—the fences half hidden, the bridges clogged, the trees laden: where the road was hard it squeaked under my feet, and where it was soft I strode through the drifts. And the air went to one's head like wine!

So I tramped past the Pattersons'. The old man, a grumpy old fellow, was going to the barn with a pail on his arm.

"Merry Christmas," I shouted.

He looked around at me wonderingly and did not reply. At the corners I met the Newton boys so wrapped in tippets that I could see only their eyes and the red ends of their small noses. I passed the Williams's house, where there was a cheerful smoke in the chimney and in the window a green wreath with a lively red bow. And I thought how happy everyone must be on a Christmas morning like this! At the hill bridge whom should I meet but the Scotch preacher himself, God bless him!

"Well, well, David," he exclaimed heartily, "Merry Christmas."

I drew my face down and said solemnly:

"Dr. McAlway, I am on a most serious errand."

"Why, now, what's the matter?" He was all sympathy at once.

"I am out in the highways trying to compel the poor of this neighborhood to come to our feast."

The Scotch preacher observed me with a twinkle in his eye.

"David," he said, putting his hand to his mouth as if to speak in my ear, "there is a poor man you will na' have to compel."

"Oh, you don't count," I said. "You're coming anyhow."

Then I told him of the errand with our millionaire friends, into the spirit of which he entered with the greatest zest. He was full of advice and much excited lest I fail to do a thoroughly competent job. For a moment I think he wanted to take the whole thing out of my hands.

"Man, man, it's a lovely thing to do," he exclaimed, "but I ha' me doots—I ha' me doots."

At parting he hesitated a moment, and with a serious face inquired:

"Is it by any chance a goose?"

"It is," I said, "a goose—a big one."

He heaved a sigh of complete satisfaction. "You have comforted my mind," he said, "with the joys of anticipation—a goose, a big goose."

So I left him and went onward toward the Starkweathers'. Presently I saw the great house standing among its wintry trees. There was smoke in the chimney but no other evidence of life. At the gate my spirits, which had been of the best all the morning, began to fail me. Though Harriet and I were well enough acquainted with the Starkweathers, yet at this late moment on Christmas morning it did seem rather a hare-brained scheme to think of inviting them to dinner.

"Never mind," I said, "they'll not be displeased to see me anyway."

I waited in the reception room, which was cold and felt damp. In the parlor beyond I could see the innumerable things of beauty—furniture, pictures, books, so very, very much of everything —with which the room was filled. I saw it now, as I had often seen it before, with a peculiar sense of weariness. How all these things, though beautiful enough in themselves, must clutter up a man's life!

Do you know, the more I look into life, the more things it seems to me I can successfully lack—and continue to grow happier. How many kinds of food I do not need, nor cooks to cook them, how much curious clothing nor tailors to make it, how many books that I never read, and pictures that are not worthwhile! The further I run, the more I feel like casting aside all such impedimenta—lest I fail to arrive at the far goal of my endeavor.

I like to think of an old Japanese nobleman I once read about, who ornamented his house with a single vase at a time, living with it, absorbing its message of beauty, and when he tired of it, replacing it with another. I wonder if he had the right way, and we, with so many objects to hang on our walls, place on our shelves, drape on our chairs, and spread on our floors, have mistaken our course and placed our hearts upon the multiplicity rather than the quality of our possessions!

Presently Mr. Starkweather appeared in the doorway. He wore a velvet smoking jacket and slippers; and somehow, for a bright morning like this, he seemed old, and worn, and cold.

"Well, well, friend," he said, "I'm glad to see you."

He said it as though he meant it.

"Come into the library; it's the only room in the whole house that is comfortably warm. You've no idea what a task it is to heat a place like this in really cold weather. No sooner do I find a man who can run my furnace then he goes off and leaves me."

"I can sympathize with you," I said, "we often have trouble at our house with the man who builds the fires."

He looked around at me quizzically.

"He lies too long in bed in the morning," I said.

By this time we had arrived at the library, where a bright fire was burning in the grate. It was a fine big room, with dark oak furnishings and books in cases along one wall, but this morning it had a disheveled and untidy look. On a little table at one side of the fireplace were the remains of a breakfast; at the other a number of wraps were thrown carelessly upon a chair. As I came in Mrs. Starkweather rose from her place, drawing a silk scarf around her shoulders. She is a robust, rather handsome woman, with many rings on her fingers, and a pair of glasses hanging to a little gold hook on her ample bosom; but this morning she, too, looked worried and old.

"Oh, yes," she said with a rueful laugh, "we're beginning a merry Christmas, as you see. Think of Christmas with no cook in the house!"

I felt as if I had discovered a gold mine. Poor starving millionaires!

But Mrs. Starkweather had not told the whole of her sorrowful story.

"We had a company of friends invited for dinner today," she said, "and our cook was ill—or said she was—and had to go. One of the maids went with her. The man who looks after the furnace disappeared on Friday, and the stableman has been drinking. We can't very well leave the place without someone who is responsible in charge of it—and so here we are. Merry Christmas!"

I couldn't help laughing. Poor people!

"You might," I said, "apply for Mrs. Heney's place."

"Who is Mrs. Heney?" asked Mrs. Starkweather.

"You don't mean to say that you never heard of Mrs. Heney!" I exclaimed. "Mrs. Heney, who is now Mrs. 'Penny' Daniels? You've missed one of our greatest celebrities."

With that, of course, I had to tell them about Mrs. Heney, who has for years performed a most important function in this community. Alone and unaided, she has been the poor whom we are supposed to have always with us. If it had not been for the devoted faithfulness of Mrs. Heney at Thanksgiving, Christmas, and other times of the year, I suppose our Woman's Aid Society and the King's Daughters would have perished miserably of undistributed turkeys and tufted comforters. For years Mrs. Heney filled the place most acceptably. Curbing the natural outpourings of a rather jovial soul, she could upon occasion look as deserving of charity as any person that ever I met. But I pitied the little Heneys: it always comes hard on the children. For weeks after every Thanksgiving and Christmas they always wore a painfully stuffed and suffocated look. I only came to appreciate fully what a self-sacrificing public servant Mrs. Heney really was when I learned that she had taken the desperate alternative of marrying "Penny" Daniels.

"So you think we might possibly aspire to the position?" laughed Mrs. Starkweather.

Upon this I told them of the trouble in our household and asked them to come down and help us enjoy

Dr. McAlway and the goose.

When I left, after much more pleasant talk, they both came with me to the door seemingly greatly improved in spirits.

"You've given us something to live for, Mr. Grayson," said Mrs. Starkweather.

60

So I walked homeward in the highest spirits, and an hour or more later whom should we see in the top of our upper field but Mr. Starkweather and his wife floundering in the snow. They reached the lane literally covered from top to toe with snow and both of them ruddy with the cold.

"We walked over," said Mrs. Starkweather breathlessly, "and I haven't had so much fun in years."

Mr. Starkweather helped her over the fence. The Scotch preacher stood on the steps to receive them, and we all went in together.

I can't pretend to describe Harriet's dinner: the gorgeous brown goose, and the apple sauce, and all the other things that best go with it, and the pumpkin pie at the end—the finest, thickest, most delicious pumpkin pie I ever ate in all my life. It melted in one's mouth and brought visions of celestial bliss. And I wish I could have a picture of Harriet presiding. I have never seen her happier, or more in her element. Every time she brought in a new dish or took off a cover it was a sort of miracle. And her coffee—but I must not and dare not elaborate.

And what great talk we had afterward!

I've known the Scotch preacher for a long time, but I never saw him in quite such a mood of hilarity. He and Mr. Starkweather told stories of their boyhood—and we laughed, and laughed—Mrs. Starkweather the most of all. Seeing her so often in her carriage, or in the dignity of her home, I didn't think she had so much jollity in her. Finally she discovered Harriet's cabinet organ, and nothing would do but she must sing for us.

"None of the newfangled ones, Clara," cried her husband: some of the old ones we used to know."

So she sat herself down at the organ and threw her head back and began to sing:

"Believe me, if all those endearing young
    charms,
Which I gaze on so fondly today—"

Mr. Starkweather jumped up and ran over to the organ and joined in with his deep voice. Harriet and I followed. The Scotch preacher's wife nodded in time with the music, and presently I saw the tears in her eyes. As for Dr. McAlway, he sat on the edge of his chair with his hands on his knees and wagged his shaggy head, and before we got through he, too, joined in with his big sonorous voice:

"Thou wouldst still be adored as this moment
    thou art—"

Oh, I can't tell you here—it grows late and there's work tomorrow—all the things we did and said. They stayed until it was dark, and when Mrs. Starkweather was ready to go, she took both of Harriet's hands in hers and said with great earnestness:

"I haven't had such a good time at Christmas since I was a little girl. I shall never forget it."

And the dear old Scotch preacher, when Harriet and I had wrapped him up, went out, saying:

"This has been a day of pleasant bread."

It has; it has. I shall not soon forget it. What a lot of kindness and common human nature—childlike simplicity, if you will—there is in people once you get them down together and persuade them that the things they think serious are not serious at all.

Unlucky Jim

Arthur S. Maxwell

Jim was the unluckiest boy who ever lived—or so he thought. Then his luck changed. Then changed back again!

Few Christmas stories have been read more than this one, beloved by generations of readers who have grown up on "Uncle Arthur's" stories. That Maxwell loved Christmas is evidenced by the 27 Christmas stories he wrote for children.

Arthur S. Maxwell (1896-1970) spent the first 40 years of his life in England and the last 34 in America. However, he never gave up his British citizenship. For 16 years he edited Present Truth *magazine, and served as editor of* Signs of the Times *magazine in America for his last 36 years.*

One of the most prolific writers of his time, altogether he wrote 112 books (79 for children and 33 for adults). They have been published in 33 countries and 37 languages. Early in his career, he began to publish value-oriented stories for children, each one based on a true incident. As a result of the escalating demand, each year for 48 consecutive years a volume of Uncle Arthur's Bedtime Stories was published, with total sales of nearly 44 million. His other continuing best selling book set, The Bible Story, *has sold to date about 27 million. All told, Maxwell's books have sold a mind-boggling 80 million copies!*

Jim thought he was the most unlucky boy that ever had been born. Everything seemed to go wrong with him. His outlook on life was particularly dark just now, for only a few minutes ago his one and only glass marble had rolled down a drain.

But quite apart from this calamity, he had much to make him feel blue. For one thing, he was shivering with cold. He should have had warm stockings and underclothes to wear, but he hadn't any, because there was not enough money to buy them. Father was out of work.

For another thing, he was hungry. It was some hours since lunch, and the bread and butter he had had then seemed to have gone clear down to the South Pole. As he trudged along the streets with his hands in his pockets, he saw lots of other boys and girls going into beautiful homes for their supper, and he knew that he would have to climb up the dirty, narrow stairs of an East End tenement for the little bit of bread and jam that he would get, for there was never enough.

Just then he passed a toy shop, all ablaze with lights and full of everything that might make a boy's heart glad. He stopped a moment and watched other boys and girls coming out with brown paper parcels under their arms. Jim jabbed his hand a little deeper down into his pocket and fingered his penny once again, his very last coin. How he wished that he could buy something to take to his little sister, lying at home so sick—something she would really like.

"If I ain't the unluckiest fellow that ever lived!" he said to himself.

But the next day his luck seemed to change. He was

walking down the street near his home when a well-dressed lady stopped him.

"Is your name Jimmie Mackay?" she asked.

"Yes, m'm," said Jimmy, surprised, and wondering what was going to happen.

"Well," said the lady, "we have your name on a list at our church, and we want you to come to a special Christmas party next week. Here is a ticket for you."

"Oh, my!" said Jimmie, not knowing what else to say. "But what about Jean—she's my sister, y' know; she'll be better by then, perhaps; she ought to come too."

"I'm afraid we can take only one from each family this time," said the lady kindly. "We will try to take Jean next time."

"Well, that's lucky and unlucky," said Jim to himself as the lady walked away. "Lucky for me and unlucky for poor Jean."

Then a bright idea occurred to him—perhaps he could let Jean go instead of him. He looked at his card. It read: "Admit bearer—Jimmie Mackay—only."

"Unlucky again!" murmured Jimmie.

So Jimmie went to the party. For the greater part of the time he forgot all about his troubles. Everything was so different, so very wonderful. He had never had so much to eat in all his life.

After supper they all played games until it was time for the presents on the Christmas tree to be given away. What excitement there was then, especially as each child was to be allowed to choose just what he wanted most.

Jim could hardly sit still as he watched the other children going up in front of him. He felt as though he were on pins and needles. He had seen such a wonderful toy fire engine hanging on the tree—something he had wanted all his life; and how he did hope and hope and *hope* that no one would ask for it first!

At last—after what seemed hours—Jimmie's turn came to make his choice.

"Jimmie Mackay!" called out the lady by the tree.

Jimmie jumped from his seat like a shell from a cannon. All he could see was the red fire engine; it was still there!

As he approached the lady he noticed that she was the very one who had spoken to him in the street and given him his ticket for the party. Immediately a new idea entered his mind.

"And what would you like to have, Jimmie?" asked

the lady. "You may have any one thing you like from the tree."

What an offer! Jimmie could scarcely take it in. He stood and gazed up at the sparkling, heavily laden tree. Once more his eye caught sight of the fire engine.

"Most of all," he said, looking up at the lady, "I would like that red fire engine; but if you don't mind, I will take that doll over there."

Tears filled his eyes as he said it, but with great resolution he kept his face straight.

Somehow the lady seemed to understand, and without a word she brought Jimmie the doll. As he went away, she squeezed his hand, and bending down, whispered, "God bless you, Jimmie."

But the other children did not understand at all. For a moment all restraint broke down, as with whoops and yells they told the world that Jimmie had chosen a doll. Some of the boys called out "Sissy!" and others, with a laugh, "Imagine a boy taking a doll!" And the little girls said, "That was just the doll we wanted!"

Jimmie blushed. He couldn't help it. Finally he became so uncomfortable that he put on his cap and went out, with the doll under his arm.

All the way home he thought about the bad luck that seemed to have dogged his footsteps that evening. First, he had lost his fire engine, and second, he had been laughed at by the whole crowd of children.

"If I'm not the unluckiest feller—" he began. Then he felt the doll under his arm. At once his thoughts brightened and his step quickened.

A few minutes later he was up in the little dark bedroom where Jean lay sick in bed.

"I'm so glad you have come!" said Jean. "It's so lonely here all by myself. And what have you got there?" she asked, sitting up in bed and peering at the doll with eager eyes. "Is that for me? Oh, Jimmie, Jimmie, you *are* a dear!"

Jimmie forgot all about his bad luck. A thrill of joy went through him as he saw his sister's delight.

Just then there was a knock at the door. It was the lady from the meeting. "What—" began Jimmie.

"I've come to say how sorry I am that the children were so unkind to you this evening," interrupted the lady. "They are sorry too, now. I told them why you chose the doll. And they asked me to bring you something for you. Here it is. Now I must go, for it is getting late. Good night!" and she was gone.

Jimmie gasped, and then opened the package.

It was the fire engine!

Then he danced a jig around Jean's bed, chuckling to himself, and saying, "If I ain't the luckiest feller that ever lived!"

Christmas Day in the Morning

Pearl Buck

What do you give to one you love very much . . . when you have nothing to give? This was the question Nobel and Pulitzer Prize Winning author Pearl Buck (see Christmas in My Heart, 2, "Stranger, Come Home") posed in this oft-reprinted little story.

For three consecutive years now, Christmas in My Heart readers have asked me to include this unforgettable story.

It is time.

* * * * *

I'll have to credit my wife, Connie, for the discovery. In all the years I had known and loved this story, I had never realized there was a longer text than the one I had always read. She had already typed the indicated text onto disk, but before going on to the next story, she was curiously shuffling through the other copies of the story in the thick folder (several having been mailed to me by readers). Then she stumbled on one that appeared to be longer than the others. Much longer!

Outside the window of our home on Maryland's Severn River, the snow was cascading lazily down in our first snowfall of the year. As she read the longer version, something began to tug at her heartstrings, and she began to choke up—it was as good as the shorter version had been, had it not been so hard to read it.

She brought it to me, knowing full well that her sentimentalist old husband would also be deeply moved. I was. Buck's early—and little known today—version has great power and is easily one of the greatest Christmas stories ever penned. The power that had been lost in the abridging has to do with a great truth: in order to give love, one must first receive such love from another. Every day in my classes, I deal with large numbers of students from broken homes. I deal with that heart-breaking reality: young men and young women unable to love because love was denied them at home—perhaps the most terrible price we pay for our user-friendly divorce laws. The price for such walk-outs is never paid: it keeps getting paid again and again as long as time lasts.

And so I thank my beloved wife Connie for her great gift to us all: Pearl Buck's original story.

He woke suddenly and completely. It was four o'clock, the hour at which his father had always called him to get up and help with the milking. Strange how the habits of his youth clung to him still! Fifty years ago, and his father had been dead for 30 years, and yet he awakened at four o'clock in the morning. He had trained himself to turn over and go to sleep, but this morning, because it was Christmas, he did not try to sleep.

Yet what was the magic of Christmas now? His childhood and youth were long past, and his own children had grown up and gone. Some of them lived only

65

a few miles away but they had their own families, and though they would come in as usual toward the end of the day, they had explained with infinite gentleness that they wanted their children to build Christmas memories about *their* houses, not his. He was left alone with his wife.

Yesterday she had said, "It isn't worth while, perhaps—"

And he had said, "Oh, yes, Alice, even if there are only the two of us, let's have a Christmas of our own."

Then she had said, "Let's not trim the tree until tomorrow, Robert—just so it's ready when the children come. I'm tired."

He had agreed, and the tree was still out in the back entry.

He lay in his big bed in his room. The door to her room was shut because she was a light sleeper, and sometimes he had restless nights. Years ago they had decided to use separate rooms. It meant nothing, they said, except that neither of them slept as well as they once had. They had been married so long that nothing could separate them, actually.

Why did he feel so awake tonight? For it was still night, a clear and starry night. No moon, of course, but the stars were extraordinary! Now that he thought of it, the stars seemed always large and clear before the dawn of Christmas Day. There was one star now that was certainly larger and brighter than any of the others. He could even imagine it moving, as it had seemed to him to move one night long ago.

He slipped back in time, as he did so easily nowadays. He was 15 years old and still on his father's farm.

He loved his father. He had not known it until one day a few days before Christmas, when he overheard what his father was saying to his mother.

"Mary, I hate to call Rob in the mornings. He's growing so fast, and he needs his sleep. If you could see how he sleeps when I go in to wake him up! I wish I could manage alone."

"Well, you can't, Adam." His mother's voice was brisk. "Besides, he isn't a child anymore. It's time he took his turn."

"Yes," his father said slowly. "But I sure do hate to wake him."

When he heard these words, something in him woke: his father loved him! He had never thought of it before, taking for granted the tie of their blood. Neither his father nor his mother talked about loving their children—they had no time for such things. There was always so much to do on a farm.

Now that he knew his father loved him, there would be no more loitering in the mornings and having to be called again. He got up after that, stumbling blind with sleep, and pulled on his clothes, his eyes tight shut, but he got up.

And then on the night before Christmas, that year when he was 15, he lay for a few minutes thinking about the next day. They were poor, and most of the excitement was in the turkey they had raised themselves and in the mince pies his mother made. His sisters sewed presents, and his mother and father always bought something he needed, not only a warm jacket, maybe, but something more, such as a book. And he saved and bought them each something, too.

He wished, that Christmas he was 15, he had a better present for his father. As usual he had gone to the ten-cent store and bought a tie. It had seemed nice enough until he lay thinking the night before Christmas, and then he wished that he had heard his father and mother talking in time for him to save for something better.

He lay on his side, his head supported by his elbow, and looked out of his attic window. The stars were bright, much brighter than he ever remembered seeing them, and one in particular was so bright he wondered if it were really the star of Bethlehem.

"Dad," he had once asked when he was a little boy, "what is a stable?"

"It's just a barn," his father had replied, "like ours."

Then Jesus had been born in a barn, and to a barn the shepherds and the Wise Men had come, bringing their Christmas gifts!

The thought struck him like a silver dagger. Why should he not give his father a special gift, too, out there in the barn? He could get up early, earlier than four o'clock, and he could creep into the barn and get all the milking done. He'd do it alone, milk and clean up, and then when his father went in to start the milking, he'd see it all done. And he would know who had done it.

He laughed to himself as he gazed at the stars. It was what he would do, and he mustn't sleep too sound.

He must have awakened 20 times, scratching a match each time to look at his old watch—midnight, and half past one, and then two o'clock.

At a quarter to three, he got up and put on his clothes. He crept downstairs, careful of the creaky boards, and let himself out. The big star hung lower over the barn roof, a reddish gold. The cows looked at him, sleepy and surprised. It was early for them too.

"So, boss," he whispered. They accepted him placidly, and he fetched some hay for each cow and then got the milking pail and the big milk cans.

He had never milked all alone before, but it seemed almost easy. He kept thinking about his father's surprise. His father would come in and call him, saying that he would get things started while Rob was getting dressed. He'd go to the barn, open the door, and then he'd go to get the two big empty milk cans. But they wouldn't be waiting or empty; they'd be standing in the milk house, filled.

"What in the world . . ." he could hear his father exclaiming.

He smiled and milked steadily, two strong streams rushing into the pail, frothing and fragrant. The cows were still surprised but acquiescent. For once they were behaving well, as though they knew it was Christmas.

The task went more easily than he had ever known it to before. Milking for once was not a chore. It was something else, a gift to his father who loved him. He finished, the two milk cans were full, and he covered them and closed the milk-house door carefully, making sure of the latch. He put the stool in its place by the door and hung up the clean milk pail. Then he went out of the barn and barred the door behind him.

Back to his room, he had only a minute to pull off his clothes in the darkness and jump into bed, for he heard his father up. He put the covers over his head to silence his quick breathing. The door opened.

"Rob!" his father called. "We have to get up, son, even if it is Christmas."

"Aw-right," he said sleepily.

"I'll go on out," his father said. "I'll get things started."

The door closed and he lay still, laughing to himself. In just a few minutes his father would know. His dancing heart was ready to jump from his body.

The minutes were endless—10, 15, he did not know how many—and he heard his father's footsteps again. The door opened and he lay still.

"Rob!"

"Yes, Dad—"

His father was laughing, a queer sobbing sort of laugh. "Thought you'd fool me, did you?" His father was standing beside his bed, feeling for him, pulling away the cover.

"It's for Christmas, Dad!"

He found his father and clutched him in a great hug. He felt his father's arms go around him. It was dark, and they could not see each other's faces.

"Son, I thank you. Nobody ever did a nicer thing—"

"Oh, Dad, I want you to know—I do want to be good!" The words broke from him of their own will. He did not know what to say. His heart was bursting with love.

"Well, I reckon I can go back to bed and sleep," his father said after a moment. "No, hark—the little ones are waked up. Come to think of it, son, I've never seen you children when you first saw the Christmas tree. I was always in the barn. Come on!"

He got up and pulled on his clothes again, and they went down to the Christmas tree; and soon the sun was creeping up to where the star had been. Oh, what a Christmas, and how his heart had nearly burst again with shyness and pride as his father told his mother and made the younger children listen about how he, Rob, had got up all by himself.

"The best Christmas gift I ever had, and I'll remember it, son, every year on Christmas morning, so long as I live."

They had both remembered it, and now that his father was dead he remembered it alone: that blessed Christmas dawn when, alone with the cows in the barn, he had made his first gift of true love.

Outside the window now the great star slowly sank. He got up out of bed and put on his slippers and bathrobe and went softly upstairs to the attic and found the box of Christmas-tree decorations. He took them downstairs into the living room. Then he brought in the tree. It was a little one—they had not had a big tree since the children went away—but he set it in the holder and put it in the middle of the long table under the window. Then carefully he began to trim it.

It was done very soon, the time passing as quickly as it had that morning long ago in the barn. He went to his library and fetched the little box that contained his special gift to his wife, a star of diamonds, not large but dainty in design. He had written the card for it the day before. He tied the gift on the tree and then stood back. It was pretty, very pretty, and she would be surprised.

But he was not satisfied. He wanted to tell her—to tell her how much he loved her. It had been a long time since he had really told her, although he loved her in a very special way, much more than he ever had when they were young.

He had been fortunate that she had loved him— and how fortunate that he had been able to love! Ah, that was the true joy of life, the ability to love! For he was quite sure that some people were genuinely unable to love anyone. But love was alive in him, it still was.

It occurred to him suddenly that it was alive because long ago it had been born in him when he knew his father loved him. That was it: love alone would waken love.

And he could give the gift again and again. This morning, this blessed Christmas morning, he would give it to his beloved wife. He could write it down in a letter for her to read and keep forever. He went to his desk and began his love letter to his wife: *My dearest love . . .*

When it was finished he sealed it and tied it on the tree where she could see it the first thing when she came into the room. She would read it, surprised and then moved, and realize how very much he loved her.

He put out the light and went tiptoeing up the stairs. The star in the sky was gone, and the first rays of the sun were gleaming the sky. Such a happy, happy Christmas!

Pink Angel

Author Unknown

When God fashioned man and woman, for some strange unexplainable reason, He instilled within each of us a yearning for appreciation. As toddlers, we grandstand from the first: "Look, Mommy! Look, Daddy!" Somehow, achievement unaccompanied by praise and recognition brings no sweeter taste than well trampled sawdust.

In this little-known old story, Christmas is coming . . . and everyone wants to be noticed at once . . . but one is not—and therein hangs the story.

There's always a special minute when it comes. Every year. Christmas, I mean.

Sometimes it's when the tree is up and trimmed and you step back from it and see it sparkle for the first time and hear it tinkling a little. And you smell that smell—of a piece of the woods brought indoors.

Sometimes it's a time when you find just the right present for someone you're very fond of and you bring it home and work over the wrapping. Or you get some special thing you never dreamed you would. Like that time I was emptying my stocking, and I saw the box underneath it move and the cover push up and two green eyes looked out and it was Magnolia, the black kitten. That was the minute that year. Often it's a song—on the radio or in church or once even the garbage man singing "Joy to the World" while he banged frozen-in grapefruit peels out of our can.

But it's always a minute that's special, and then Christmas is there. It's come for you. It hits you and leaves bells ringing in your ears.

It came twice for me that year. The first time was on a Thursday, and we had only the next week and a half to go before vacation.

I had been feeling low ever since after Thanksgiving when they gave out the parts for the Christmas program. My brother Pud came home all hepped up over getting a speaking part in his school play. My little brother Bumps was going to be one of the three kings of Orient. Even my tiny sister—she was going to be an angel in the Benjamin School play. Four rooms in her school and a little 5-year-old kid gets a solo part! I'm the dumb one. The big brother in junior high, that's me. I get nothing.

Mother glowed when they told her. That's a nice thing about Mother. If you do something good, you sure get appreciation.

"Just think!" she said. "Such smart children I have. Some people have *one* smart one, one that gets into things. Look at me. Every single one. Jean, singing a whole verse of 'Away in a Manger' all by herself. King Balthazar Bumps, Innkeeper Pud." She looked at me. "And Rod," she said.

I laughed. "Yeah," I said, "and Rod."

"Well," Mother said, "playing in the orchestra isn't

70

to be sneezed at. Playing a trumpet in an orchestra is fully as important as anything else," she said. But she swelled her voice too much on it. She was feeling sorry for me. She was proud of the others. She was sorry for me.

So it was her face lighting up that I saw on Thursday when Miss Phelps told me. Even before I got home, before I ever told her, that's what I could see. Mother's face glowing with pride. Christmas had come. Only this time it didn't last.

It began to snow on the way home, and that made everything perfect. I ran the last block. I would have flown if I could fly. Snow for Christmas and me with the lead in the Christmas play! I couldn't wait to tell it. I wouldn't wait. Would Mother's eyes shine! It was too bad about Jim having to go to California, but *me!*

I stood for a minute by the door, watching the snow, catching flakes on my tongue, trying to get myself quiet before I went in. I didn't want Mother to think I cared so much. I wanted to sound like it wasn't so much, me getting the lead.

I'd have to get a shepherd costume, a sheepskin thing they wanted, but Mother would do that. She was good at things like that.

"We must have a sheepskin someplace," she'd say, "under some of this junk around here," she'd say and her eyes would be shining at me, hardly believing it. . . . She'd pooh-pooh the costume. "I'll get one," she'd say. "My goodness, for the boy with the biggest part in the play, we'll find a costume. We'll *buy* a sheep and *skin* it if we have to," she'd say. "Just you leave it to me."

I took a big gulp of the Christmas air and went in.

"Our program's Wednesday afternoon," I said. Just casual. Nobody knew I was the star.

"Wednesday," Mother said. "That's the twenty-first," She was piling cookies into a can. "Here, take one," she said.

It crumbled when I bit it. Pecans inside.

A lock of hair was in Mother's eyes, and she pushed it away with her arm. She looked tired. She said, "Rod, can you come right home after school and stay with Jean?"

"Yeah, I guess so," I said. "Unless we have to practice." I took a big breath. "You see," I said, trying not to act excited, "I—"

"That's good," Mother said. "I've simply got to go downtown. There's Mable and Lucile I haven't even looked for presents for yet. And Jeanie's presents for the neighborhood children. I'll have to take her along for that. And I haven't any of the family presents yet."

"I have a lot to do, Mother," I said.

"I know," Mother said. "Everybody's busy. It's getting so that's all there is to Christmas anymore. Rush, rush, rush. I hope Father can address cards tonight. He just has to take that over. When you come home, Rod, stop in at Rich's and see if you can get a box that would fit that stuff." She nodded to a chair full of packages in the corner. "I have to get that stuff off right away, or it'll never get there for Christmas. Just think! Only two weeks away. It drives me crazy when I think of it."

About a week for me. A week to learn that part! It kinda drove me crazy too.

"Mother," I said, "I need a lot of time myself for—" but she was putting the can of cookies out on the back porch and talking.

"But not this noon," she was saying. "There's salad in the refrigerator. Get it out, will you?" She came back in and started putting dishes on the table. "We don't really have time to eat anymore," she said. "Where are Bumps and Pud anyway? Look out the window, Rod, and see what's keeping them. Jean, get your bib on and start eating. I should start you at eleven-thirty, the way you dawdle."

I gave up trying to tell her then. A thing like that you can't blurt out. I called my brothers.

They came in and dropped their jackets, and Bumps said, "I'll have to have that king of Orient's costume, you know."

Mother sighed and dried her hands on the towel by the sink. "Butter a roll for Jean, Rod," she said. "What do kings of Orient wear? Bright colors, mostly, I guess. I'll look in the trunk. I know!" she said then. "Maybe I can borrow that bright blue flannel peignoir of Barbara's and work it from there."

"What's a peignoir?" Bumps said. "I'm not going to wear girl's clothes!"

"It's a robe," Mother said. "Kings have to wear robes. Don't worry. I'll figure out something real kingly. I always do, don't I? Why couldn't you have been one of the singers—in everyday clothes? Why did you all have to be so talented, you smart children you!" She grinned. "Making so much work! I have to think up king's costumes while I'm pushing through crowds looking for some nice little thing for the woman who was so nice to us last summer."

My, she didn't have time to listen to me tell about getting the lead, much less find a costume for me! You couldn't help being sorry Mother was so busy she had to eat on the run. But it made you kind of mad too. That she had to be so busy when you had such an important thing to tell. So busy she couldn't stop long enough to hear. My—this was big stuff! This was *big*. Not just a verse of a song. Not just a speaking part, not just a king of Orient. This was the *lead*.

"You didn't have to send that woman up north a present," I said. "You didn't have to."

"Well, I want to," Mother said. "But it's that angel costume for Jean which has me whirling right this minute. Angel costume, indeed. They're balmy over at that school."

Jean's lip shook a little, and she pushed a piece of pear around with her fork. Mother was pouring hot water over her tea bag in her cup. She put the kettle back on the stove quick and patted Jean's shoulder.

"Oh, don't worry, darling. I'll do 'er," Mother said. "I'll do 'er up brown."

"Not brown," said Jean unsteadily. "Pink."

"Yeah, pink," Mother said. "You'll be the angelest angel in town. Just you push some salad into that angel mouth."

Jean's eyes were shining wet, and she ate a big bite of salad.

"I know my part," she said. Her eyes were almost dancing out of her head! For Jean it was now. It was the first time. As long as I live I'll never forget that first time for me in kindergarten. The Magic Star-maker, that was me. I remembered, looking at Jean, how wonderful I felt when I came home and told it; how it was, that day. A sea of faces with clapping hands beneath them. And Mother in the second row. That's the way it would be for Jean. The Christmas tree would sparkle in the corner, the people would smell wintery and Christmasy, the excitement would be racing all around, and she'd be good and Mother would be watching! Oh, it's always wonderful, but the first time it's magic.

"I know it perfeck," Jean said. "Want to hear it?"

"Darling, I can't hear it too often," Mother said, and Jean dropped her fork and stood on her chair and sang it, bobbing her head with the rhythm of it, her long blond hair bouncing, her eyes big and dark and serious.

> "The cat-tle are low-ing the poor baby wakes
> But lit-tle Lord Je-sus, no cry-ing He makes.
> I love Thee, Lord Je-sus, look down from
>   the sky
> And stay by my cra-dle till morning is nigh."

Sure hits the down beat, Jean does.

"Oh, it's so wunnerful," she said. "Wasn't I lucky to get pink for my angel suit, Mother? They pulled the colors out of a box, and Alice got blue and Gail got white and pink was left for me and that's best." I guess we'd heard about it a hundred times, but Jean was still telling it with gusto. Mother was listening with gusto too, her face beaming at Jean.

So I decided to wait. I decided not to tell Mother my big news till later, till she wasn't so busy that having to find a shepherd costume would be the last straw. I'd wait till I was alone with her so I could have all that gloating for me alone.

Mother gathered up her dishes and put them in the sink and sat Jean down again. She kissed the top of her head. "Eat the lettuce," she said. "You're going to have an angel suit that'll knock their eyes out. You know what I found this morning? An old pink formal I had once. You're going to be a stiff little pink tulle angel, darling. Finish eating and I'll show you. Tonight we'll cut it out. It isn't the gown that worries me, it's those wings. But we'll figure it out. Do you know your part, Bumps?"

Did he know his part? Wait'll she heard about me. The whole lead to learn in a week.

"Sure," Bumps said. "I just walk. Step and hold, step and hold. It's easy. You got something for the murr?"

"The murr?" Mother said.

"Yeah," said Bumps. "You know, 'Murr is mine its bitter perfume breathes a life of gathering bloom sawring sighing bleeding dying sealed in a stone-cold tomb oh oh!'"

"Oh, myrrh," Mother said. "No, I haven't. But I'll look around. Goodness, you make it mournful. Don't you know how to sing it?"

"I don't sing it," Bumps said. "I just march it."

"What?" Mother said, surprised. "I thought it was your rich voice you were picked for, but you just march it? It was your gorgeous physique and kingly carriage you got chosen for—well, well. And your costume—resourceful Mother, perhaps. Pud, you stop at Benson's shop for sure and get that cloak you're going to wear so I can wash it tonight. Oh, Rod, you are a comfort to me! I like people whose talents run to playing trumpets in school orchestras in plain suits of clothes."

"Well,"—it wasn't exactly a good opening for it, but: "Mother, I'm not going to play in the orchestra," I said.

"Oh," Mother said. A sharp little oh. "That's too bad," she said. "But don't you care, Rod. It's fun just to sit and watch. We have to have watchers too. We have to have an audience or there couldn't be any programs."

"Well, I'm not going to—" I began, but just then Jean stood up and handed her plate across to Mother.

"See, I cleaned it up," she said. "I better practice my part again, Mother."

"Oh, you know that thing frontwards and backwards," Bumps said.

"I do not," Jean said. "We have to march too. We have to march up when they play the piano. You can't go too fast. 'The cat-tle are low-ing the poor baby wakes—'"

Suddenly I saw red. What if she was little, what if I was the oldest? Mother was my Mother too. Why couldn't I even have a chance to tell her about me?

"Oh, keep still a minute!" I said. "Mother! I'm not going to watch!"

"Rod!" Mother said. "Let her practice her part! My goodness, it takes practice to march and sing like an angel." And then she lowered her voice. "She's little, darling, let her enjoy it. Remember how it is the first time."

"Sure," I said. I could wait. My news would blow her over when it came. I could wait.

I worked on it while I was staying with Jean. And by dinnertime I just about knew it. Mother came home with Father, both of them loaded with packages, Mother's face sagging with tiredness. She sank into a chair and kicked off her shoes and closed her eyes.

"Poor Father," she said. "If I had to battle that streetcar gang every night, I'd give up. Get my slippers, Pud. Get Father's slippers."

"It's not quite that bad all the time," Father said.

"I'd like to fall into bed," Mother said, "without undressing. Thank goodness for automatic ovens anyway. We come home, open the magic door and there it is—meat loaf and scalloped potatoes. All we have to do is set the table."

"That's wonderful," Father said. "I'll have to learn that trick. What number do you set it at to get turkey?"

"There's a little more to it than that," Mother said. "But I do have one trick I'm going to need you for tonight. I'll show you how. All you have to do is sit in the chair by the desk and put a pen between your thumb and forefinger and turn your back to us. There's a list and a pile of envelopes and in about three hours time, presto—addressed Christmas cards all ready to go!"

I stacked the dishes and went to my room to study. I studied my part. As soon as the kids went to bed I'd tell her. And when I told her, I'd know it. She could hold the book while I'd say it over. Nothing nice and average about me. I get a lead in the morning, by night

I know it. I was doing it in front of the mirror without the book when I heard her call.

"Everyone!" she called. "Hey, come and look. Just come and look!"

Pud ran down ahead of me, and Bumps came banging out of the bathroom. Father had come from the study and stood with his pen in his hand. Mother was in the middle of the floor, and there were pink threads and scissors and pins in a box and over at the far end of the living room was Jean.

My breath stopped. And for a second it was all pure Christmas—something you can't quite keep but only can remember a little. There was Jean, a fluffy pink glittering angel, too beautiful to believe. It went straight from the neck, the gown, clear down to her ankles, and her arms were lost in it and it was like pink foam, like glistening spun sugar, ready to disappear; and floating above it, with sparkling wings just showing in back, Jeanie's wide-eyed face. I never knew she was that pretty. All creamy pink and her mouth a little open and her eyes round and big and dark and her hair a soft golden crown around her head.

"My, that's pretty!" Bumps said.

And Pud said, "Wowie!"

And Father said, "Oh Honey, don't look so beautiful or someone's going to steal you away from us!"

And Mother said, "Isn't she darling?"

And Jean put one hand over her mouth and drew in her breath in a little gaspy delighted laugh and wriggled her shoulders, and then Father said, "I'll get the lights, I'll get the camera, we have to have a picture of that!" Father took the picture and then my world went spinning.

"Couldn't they let you off from work, Father?" Jean asked. "Couldn't they let you off for a good program like that? It's gonna be awful good!"

"I don't know but they might," Father said. "I don't know but they'd almost have to. When is this affair?"

"It's two o'clock," Jean said, "but we have to come ahead of time. Two o'clock Wednesday," Jean said.

"Of course, Wednesday. There isn't any school on Thursday, silly." Mother unfastened the angel gown and pulled it up over Jean's head.

"Wednesday?" I said, standing real still. "The twenty-first?" I said.

"Yup," Jean said, pulling her undershirt down over her stomach. "Wednesday, December the twenty-first at two p.m., and everybody better get there early to get a good seat. You better get there early, Mother, and then you can sit right in front."

Mother smiled down at her. "Hurry now," she said. "It's past bedtime for all of you. What's the matter with you, Rod? Don't stand there dreaming. It's late."

I followed them upstairs. I went to my room and closed the door. I put the copy of the play in the drawer of my desk and locked the drawer. It was a long time before I could get to sleep.

We practiced every morning before school. We practiced every day during school. We practiced sometimes after school. By the end of the next week I knew it frontwards and backwards. I knew it sideways. I knew the leading part of the play in less than a week with nobody helping me. I knew it, but it wasn't any good. Nobody was going to see me. Why should I care? Who cares if I'm any good?

It was the way they had schools in our town. All of us in different schools, that was why. They didn't plan it for people who had more than one child. Jean went to Benjamin. Me, I went to junior high. What did they care about people who had kids in Benjamin and West Side? People weren't supposed to have kids a lot of different ages. What did they care if the programs came the same day, the same hour? What was that to them?

I couldn't even tell her about the costume. I didn't know what to do about that. Maybe I was a softy, but I couldn't do that to Jean. I'd look at her at mealtime, jabbering away about their program, jabbery-happy, and I'd think about it. I'd think about how it would be if I was to say, "Hey, Mom, I've got the lead in our Christmas play. I've got the lead, Mom." I don't know how it would have come out. I don't know what Mother could have done about it. If she came to see me it would

break Jeanie's heart. I knew that. If she didn't come—it was better for Mother not to know about it at all than to have to know and not come. I kept still.

So on Monday Miss Phelps says I'm no good. "I thought you were better than Jim had been," she said. "You read it so well that first day. What's happened to you? Please try harder," she said. "Try to think how you'd feel if you were that shepherd boy who had to stay behind when the others went to Bethlehem. You're the one that's left out, the one that nothing big can happen to. Try to make it feel like that."

"OK," I said. What did they expect of a just-average kid? What did they expect?

"And you'll have to have that costume by tomorrow," she said.

"OK," I said.

I didn't care what I wore. I went up in the attic at noon and looked in the trunk. So, who cared what the shepherd boy wore? Who cared anyway? Sheepskin. What did they think? That people just had sheepskin lying around their houses?

There wasn't anything in the trunk. Satin dresses, striped pants, silk scarves. I bundled the junk all up and rammed it back in and closed the lid. It was cold up there in the attic but I didn't care. I dropped down on the rug in front of the trunk and put my head on my arm, face down. Maybe I'd catch cold so I couldn't be in the play. I didn't care. Christmas sure was a lot of bother and work. That's the way it is, I guess, when you grow up. I was getting old, was all. It's kind of tough, outgrowing Christmas.

Can't blame a kid for crying when he gets that blue.

I felt better after a while. I sat up and wiped my eyes on my sweater and waited a few minutes before I went down so my eyes wouldn't be red. Mother thought I was hiding Christmas presents or something up there. It sure was cold. I couldn't find a shepherd costume and I didn't care. Maybe they'd take the part away from me. I shrugged my shoulders and put the rug up around my legs to keep then warm.

It was an old fur rug made from the hide of a cow or something, that Grandpa got once. I stood up and picked up the rug—it was just the thing! All I needed was a hole for my head. I took it down to my room and cut one and tried it on. It looked kind of sad after all, but I sneaked it out to school anyway. It sort of covered me up at least.

The teacher fastened it together at the sides and between the legs with staples. "Guess it'll have to do," she said. "It certainly doesn't look like a sheepskin, though." She sure looked worried. What was so important? Nobody was going to see it.

"Sometimes sheep are black," I said.

"Yes, I know," Miss Phelps said. "But this is brown—or red. Are you sure it was a cow? It has such long hair. And sheep are curly."

"Maybe it's a buffalo from the Western prairies," I said.

"If it was a buffalo," she said, "it must have died of old age. Well, cow or buffalo, it'll just have to do. You aren't supposed to look glamorous after all."

I certainly didn't. I sort of looked like an old buffalo getting ready to die with its hide getting too loose for its frame. I felt like one too.

We got the Christmas tree up that night, and I could almost feel happy again, just looking at it. Every reddish-pink ball made me think of Jean in the angel costume. I was sure glad I hadn't spoiled it for Jean. After all, Christmas is for kids.

On Tuesday, Mother went to the West Side to see Bumps march the king of Orient and carry the myrrh in an old Chinese brass pot she'd borrowed and to hear Pud say his two lines. "They were wonderful," she told Father that night. "Just wonderful! Aren't we lucky to have such gifted children?" she said. "Bumps was kingly and steady and—inspired looking. I was proud of him."

Bumps beamed. "It sure was hard to walk that slow," he said.

"I'll bet," Mother said. "And Pud was wonderful! You'd have thought he really owned that inn. You were wonderful, Pud."

"That's what everybody said," said Pud.

"And now tomorrow is Jean," she said. "My goodness, what would I do if I had eight children? I couldn't take it, I'd be so worn out running from one program to another." Suddenly Mother stopped talking. "Rod!" she said. "I forgot. Oh, Rod! I forgot all about you. Have I missed it? What day is your program? I completely forgot."

"That's OK," I said. "It's tomorrow. You can't go to both."

"Oh, Rod," Mother said. "I did so want to hear you play in the orchestra. Oh, what am I going to do?" You should have seen Jean—she looked like the end of the world.

"Well, you have to go and see Jean," I said, and it was worth it seeing her come alive again. "Anyway," I said, "I'm not going to play in that old orchestra."

Mother sank back in her chair. "I don't know, Rod," she said. "You always do things right somehow. Every mother ought to have a child like you. You never complicate things; you never foul things up. You always make things come out right, and I love you. You'll play in the orchestra for the spring concert, I know you will; and we'll all go to hear you. Wouldn't you like to stay out and come and see Jean be an angel? I'll write you an excuse. Why don't you?"

"I'd better go to ours," I said simply.

"That's right," Mother said. "That's right. You had better. We wouldn't want anyone to think you were jealous or anything because you didn't get chosen to play with the orchestra this time."

Rod, you always do things right somehow. I kept thinking about Mother saying that, when I was getting my cow skin on.

The teacher was extra-excited. "Please do your best," she said to me. "Do it the way you did that first day, the day you read it. Make it good, Rod," she said, "and then maybe they won't notice your costume. I wonder if it would help any to trim off some of that hair." So she tried it. It gave it more of a French poodle look, and Miss Phelps looked sad and said pleadingly, "Do your best, Rod, please."

OK, I will, I thought. *I'm the one that always does things right somehow.*

It wasn't hard, I'll say that. It wasn't hard to act it. It was just the way I felt. I just acted me, the way I felt upstairs there in the attic the day I found the cow skin. I was getting too old for Christmas. That was for kids. I

was left behind now. Left behind while Jean and Bumps and Pud went ahead and had Christmas. Left behind while the others went to Bethlehem to see the Baby King in the manger. I was the shepherd boy who'd had to get his own costume, who was left behind to tend the sheep so the others could go. My, it wasn't hard at all.

I even got weepy over it. Nobody wants to be left behind while others go on and see the miracle. Nobody wants to grow up, I guess, and take responsibilities, give up things so others can have them. It wasn't hard and I was doing it! I was doing it like a breeze. I threw myself into it, moth-eaten old cow skin and all. And I knew I was good.

I could see Miss Phelps in the wings. Poor Miss Phelps. I'd sure let her down until now. Her face looked droopy and ready to cry. Miss Phelps was dead on her feet, she was too tired and nervous. She'd had to wait through all the orchestra playing, through all the carol singing, nervous because I was such a flop. Now she could hardly believe it. I was good.

I felt sorry for Miss Phelps. She was like me. Nobody cared enough to help her. Until now, I hadn't seen her side of it. Well, I was grown up now. I had to think about those things. It was a sad thing to miss out on Christmas, but you didn't need to spoil it for others.

Only I'd had that little cry when nobody was looking. Up in the attic on the cow skin. And I could cry here in the pasture after the others had gone and I knew I had missed out. I pillowed my head on my arm in the grass of the stage pasture and cried. It came easy. The rest might not be so easy, but the crying was. Next came the hard part. In a minute I'd hear the quartet singing softly up in the rafters: "Peace on earth—" and then would come the hard part. Then I'd have to raise my head in wonder and let it show in my face.

Out of the dusky background on a raised place, lights would come up on the nativity scene. The shepherd boy would see it after all, and I'd have to show how wonderful he felt about it. I hadn't done it right yet. I'd been told often enough. I just couldn't make Nancy and Timmy seem wonderful enough to get all excited over. Not even all dressed up in Bible clothes and leaning over the manger with tableau lights and a fine screen in front of them. Not even with the wonderful animals Perry'd gotten from his father's market. Not even when the shepherds came and the wise men came. Not even in costume. I guess I'm just not made that way. I just kept trying to figure out whose bathrobe they were wearing.

Then I sat up like a shot. Something was goofy. Someone was patting my head! I sat up and turned around and I didn't need to act to look surprised. To look dumbfounded! A glistening pink angel was patting my head, and my mouth dropped open, and I was dumbfounded.

Jean!

And that's when Christmas came the second time. That's when the glory hit me. Hit me with a bang that burst my eardrums, with a blaze that split my eyeballs.

For just one second I looked everywhere because it was too much for me. I just couldn't get it. And afterward they said that was good. As if I was wondering where the music had come from, where the angel had come from.

And I saw Mother!

She was standing in the wings beside Miss Phelps.

Was she ever glowing! Maybe she was proud of Jean and Pud and Bumps. She was super-proud of me. Not just because I had the lead. That was small stuff compared to the other. She was proud of me for not spoiling it for Jean. She smiled a wonderful smile, and she motioned with her eyes, and I took Jeanie's hand and turned and looked at the tableau, and if that audience couldn't see the glory shining in my face, they must be blind. It was blinding me.

Sometimes I think that's the peak. I'll probably never again have Christmas hit me like that. Right between the eyes. I hardly heard Mother explaining how Jean's program wasn't very long and she felt badly about me being the left-out one and so she'd gathered her up, wings and all, and had come on over. How they'd told her then, and let them stand in the wings. How wonderful I'd acted, so wonderful that Jean had been taken in and had run to comfort me.

I was still standing there when they all crowded around, squealing and jumping and Miss Phelps crying and telling me our play was going to be put on at the museum—with the sheepskin lining of an old coat of Father's instead of the cow skin, Mother said, and even with Jean. Most people thought it was planned that way, with Jean.

It didn't worry me any. I could do it again. With Mother watching, I could do it easy. I was grown up, I was good, and the bells were ringing in my head.

Maybe Christmas will come again like that some day. But it can never be the same. That will always be the peak—the year I grew up and got hit so hard with the glory of Christmas.

Christmas Lost and Found

Shirley Barksdale

It was not a good Christmas, that year. Their Christmas boy had come to them on Christmas—and left them on Christmas.

"Without his invincible yuletide spirit, we were like poorly trained dancers, unable to perform after the music had stopped."

But now, 16 years after they had fled all their son had known and loved, they had returned. Why, they really didn't know. But here they were.

And then they heard the screech of car brakes . . .

This little story, born in a 1988 McCalls, *and quickly picked up by* Reader's Digest, *has become, for many, a cherished Christmas tradition.*

We called him our Christmas Boy, because he came to us during that season of joy, when he was just 6 days old. Already his eyes twinkled more brightly than the lights on his first tree.

Later, as our family expanded, he made it clear that only he had the expertise to select and decorate the tree each year. He rushed the season, starting his gift list before we'd even finished the Thanksgiving turkey. He pressed us into singing carols, our croaky voices sounding more froglike than ever compared to his perfect pitch. He stirred us up, led us through a round of merry chaos.

Then, on his twenty-fourth Christmas, he left us as unexpectedly as he had come. A car accident, on an icy Denver street, on his way home to his young wife and infant daughter. But first he had stopped by the family home to decorate our tree, a ritual he had never abandoned.

Without his invincible yuletide spirit, we were like poorly trained dancers, unable to perform after the music had stopped. In our grief, his father and I sold our home, where memories clung to every room. We moved to California, leaving behind our support system of friends and church. All the wrong moves.

It seemed I had come full circle, back to those early years when there had been just my parents and me. Christmas had always been a quiet, hurried affair, unlike the celebrations at my friends' homes, which were lively and peopled with rollicking relatives. I vowed then that someday I'd marry and have six children, and that at Christmas my house would vibrate with energy and love.

I found the man who shared my dream, but we had not reckoned on the surprise of infertility. Undaunted, we applied for adoption, ignoring gloomy prophecies that an adopted child would not be the same as "our own flesh and blood." Even then, hope did not run high; the waiting list was long. But against all odds, within a year he arrived and was ours. Then nature sur-

prised us again, and in rapid succession we added two biological children to the family. Not as many as we had hoped for, but compared to my quiet childhood, three made an entirely satisfactory crowd.

Those friends were right about adopted children not being the same. He wasn't the least like the rest of us. Through his own unique heredity, he brought color into our lives with his gift of music, his irrepressible good cheer, his bossy wit. He made us look and behave better than we were.

In the 16 years that followed his death, time added chapters to our lives. His widow remarried and had a son; his daughter graduated from high school. His brother married and began his own Christmas traditions in another state. His sister, an artist, seemed fulfilled by her career. His father and I grew old enough to retire, and in December of 1987 we decided to return to Denver. The call home was unclear; we knew only that we yearned for some indefinable connection, for something lost that had to be retrieved before time ran out.

We slid into Denver on the tail end of a blizzard. Blocked highways forced us through the city, past the Civic Center, ablaze with thousands of lights—a scene I was not ready to face. This same trek had been one of our Christmas Boy's favorite holiday traditions. He had been relentless in his insistence that we all pile into the car, its windows fogged over with our warm breath, its tires fighting for a grip in ice.

I looked away from the lights and fixed my gaze on the distant Rockies, where he had loved to go barreling up the mountainside in search of the perfect tree. Now in the foothills there was his grave—a grave I could not bear to visit.

Once we were settled in the small, boxy house, so different from the family home where we had orchestrated our lives, we hunkered down like two barn swallows who had missed the last migration south. While I stood staring toward the snowcapped mountains one day, I heard the sudden screech of car brakes, then the impatient peal of the doorbell. There stood our granddaughter, and in the gray-green eyes and impudent grin I saw the reflection of our Christmas Boy.

Behind her, lugging a large pine tree, came her mother, stepfather, and 9-year-old half brother. They swept past us in a flurry of laughter; they uncorked the sparkling cider and toasted our homecoming. Then they decorated the tree and piled gaily wrapped packages under the boughs.

81

"You'll recognize the ornaments," said my former daughter- in-law. "They were his. I saved them for you."

"I picked out most of the gifts, Grandma," said the 9-year-old, whom I hardly knew.

When I murmured, in remembered pain, that we hadn't had a tree for, well, 16 years, our cheeky granddaughter said, "Then it's time to shape up!"

They left in a whirl, shoving one another out the door, but not before asking us to join them the next morning for church, then dinner at their home.

"Oh, we just can't," I began.

"You sure can," ordered our granddaughter, as bossy as her father had been. "I'm singing the solo, and I want to see you there."

"Bring earplugs," advised the 9-year-old.

We had long ago given up the poignant Christmas services, but now, under pressure, we sat rigid in the front pew, fighting back tears.

Then it was solo time. Our granddaughter swished (her father would have swaggered) to center stage, and the magnificent voice soared, clear and true, in perfect pitch. She sang "O Holy Night," which brought back bittersweet memories. In a rare emotional response, the congregation applauded in delight. How her father would have relished that moment!

We had been alerted that there would be a "whole mess of people" for dinner—but 35? Assorted relatives filled every corner of the house; small children, noisy and exuberant, seemed to bounce off the walls. I could not sort out who belonged to whom, but it didn't matter. They all belonged to one another. They took us in, enfolded us in joyous camaraderie. We sang carols in loud, off-key voices, saved only by that amazing soprano.

Sometime after dinner, before the winter sunset, it occurred to me that a true family is not always one's own flesh and blood. It is a climate of the heart. Had it not been for our adopted son, we would not now be surrounded by caring strangers who would help us to hear the music again.

Later, not yet ready to give up the day, our granddaughter asked us to come along with her. "I'll drive," she said. "There's a place I like to go." She jumped behind the wheel of the car and, with the confidence of a newly licensed driver, zoomed off toward the foothills.

Alongside the headstone rested a small, heart-shaped rock, slightly cracked, painted by our artist daughter. On its weathered surface she had written: "To my brother, with love." Across the crest of the grave lay a holly-bright Christmas wreath. Our number-two son admitted, when asked, that he sent one every year.

In the chilly but somehow comforting silence, we were not prepared for our unpredictable granddaughter's next move. Once more that day her voice, so like her father's, lifted in song, and the mountainside echoed the chorus of "Joy to the World," on and on into infinity.

When the last pure note had faded, I felt, for the fist time since our son's death, a sense of peace, of the positive continuity of life, of renewed faith and hope. The real meaning of Christmas had been restored to us. Hallelujah!

A Doll From Muzzy

Penny Estes Wheeler

What is it about babydolls that makes us love them so? Certainly God must smile to look down on little girls playing "Mother," unconsciously preparing for the day when flesh and blood replaces porcelain. No more daunting task faces a mortal than to raise a child. But, to have loved dolls in childhood is to have filled one's heart with such a storehouse of love that a lifetime is too short a space in which to empty it.

(Penny Estes Wheeler, a widely published author, is the Review and Herald Acquisitions Editor who encouraged me to produce the Christmas in My Heart series. She has since taken on another role, editor-in-chief of a new woman's magazine, Women of Spirit. Not long ago she sent me a copy of a family treasure, her 1970 Christmas letter/gift to her parents and family. Eerily, she had titled it "Christmas in My Heart!" The lead story has to do with her adored mother, Muzzy, who lit up the world with her magnetic field, her all-embracing love. She passed away 19 years ago, laments my editor friend, and oh, how she is missed! But in this heartfelt story, Muzzy lives on.)

Oh, what a *little* girl I was in the first Christmas of my memory! The small living room in the duplex was transformed into a magical place, because in front of the window stood a real pine tree. Bright balls and silver icicles adorned it, and an angel fluttered upon the topmost branch.

Underneath the tree, ah, the greatest wonder of it all! Bright-papered boxes of all shapes and sizes rested in secret silence, awaiting The Day.

All silent, but one box. Even then I must have loved rearranging packages, because as I stacked them and shook them, I heard a strange squeak inside one long box.

"Maybe it's a mouse," someone told me. Who said it, I don't know, for I'm sure I pestered everyone with the mystery.

Time passes, as it must, and Christmas morning our whole family crowded into the living room. Our group included Daddy and Muzzy (my mother), Mama (my grandmother), PaPa (my grandfather), and baby sister, Judye. After what had seemed like months of waiting, the bright boxes were finally given to their owners. The box with the mouse trapped inside was handed to me.

Scared of mice, I was afraid to open the box. "Come stand close to me," PaPa said. "If a mouse runs out, I'll step on it."

And I, looking up at his tall, thin frame, nodded in trusting agreement. "PaPa'll step on it."

So creeping close to him, I bravely opened the lid and found a dolly sleeping among white tissue. My first doll. The first in a procession that didn't end until

Mama gave each of us a baby doll after we were in college, and then Judye gave me one that kicked and cried until a bottle was put in its mouth.

Mama was excited about the dolls she gave us when we were grown. "You've got to see this doll," she told me, as we were on our way to do some Christmas shopping. "It looks just like a real baby and feels like one in your arms."

So we went to the toy store and sure enough the doll lay soft and limp in her box, awaiting a new mother. We cuddled it, laughing as we lay it against our shoulders and felt its rounded bottom against our sheltering arms. Just like a real baby.

I went back and bought the doll—Johanna—for Mama. For Christmas. And when we opened our shoe boxes that morning we found that Johanna's twin baby sisters nestled inside.

Between the first and the last dolls marched a procession of doll babies unequaled in love bestowed upon them by their child mother. Oh, how I loved my dolls!

Judye wanted a Toni doll that year, the year that I begged for a doll that looked like a real baby. She got her Toni (a silly little thing with hair that you could actually curl), and I got Nancy Sue. She lay in her box, a vision of old-time babyhood with her brown, painted hair and long, pink christening gown. I cherished her, that baby with the soft cloth body and hard arms and legs. She couldn't sit up or talk or dance or splash or even drink and wet or take a bath. All she could do was lie there and be loved. And love her I did.

I was a little older when I fell in love with "Baby Coo." My cousin Tess had one. Two girls in Wyatt's cafeteria—where we ate now and then—stood in line with theirs. I could hardly believe it. "Baby Coo" looked *real!* They cost a lot. Too much, I'm sure. But I begged for one. Promised wild and impossible things if I'd only be given one. My aunt had a soft, pink new baby to rock and feed and play with. The next best thing, to my thinking, was the wonderful, lifelike "Baby Coo."

You guessed it. I named her Isobel and will never forget her. I dressed her in real baby clothes—cloth diapers and rubber pants, baby booties and gowns, and bonnets. When we went on vacation I left her with my young boy cousin who fed her damp cookies that stuck to her face. I bathed her and powdered her, dressed and undressed her until she literally fell apart at her rubber seams.

I took her to camp meeting with me. Big, soft, huggable—she was my all-time favorite. And when I take her ancient, taped-up body from her storage bed today, I love her still.

"Will we get a doll this time?" That was the question I breathlessly asked each year. *What did girls get who didn't get dolls? I wondered. What could they want besides dolls? What did you do when you "outgrew" dolls? What did you play with? How could anyone be happy at Christmas without a new doll?*

The dolls kept coming. Little ones and larger ones. Some had painted heads; some wore wigs. Years ago doll hair was not rooted as it is today, and painted hair had the advantage that it didn't come unglued. Their cheeks were rosy. Some had tiny pearl-like teeth between ruby lips. Some were pale-skinned, some brown-skinned. I loved them all.

At last Muzzy announced that we were too big for

dolls. I didn't want to believe it. Not that I actually *played* dolls with the dedication of years before, but I couldn't imagine Christmas without one. The evidence was strong, however. No long, rectangular boxes rested under the Christmas tree. No doll boxes. No dolls.

There was one big, tall, long box. It was actually two boxes taped together, and if I hadn't been so honorable or so dumb I might have guessed, but I was.

"Don't pick up that box," Muzzy told us. "Something might break." The tag read, *to Penny and Judye,* and I should have known . . .

But if I'd been smarter, I would not have experienced the pleasure of surprise as the opened box revealed the biggest doll ever, with yellow curls and a pink organdy dress. Two dolls, actually, wrapped one atop the other. I named mine Elizabeth and played with her until her curls became ragged, her soft arms darkened, and her rosy cheeks grew scratched and faded.

Oh, how we played dolls! We had miniature baby beds with pink air mattresses and up-and-down railings. They were perfect for our sleeping babies. Daddy let us have half of the garage. With the help of two neighborhood girls, we painted the walls, arranged old furniture, put the babies' beds in place, and enjoyed a unique combination of mother role playing with our doll babies and preteen girl talk.

The "Toodles" dolls were the final ones we received. I was in the eighth-grade, much too old to pretend motherhood, to pretend to put baby to sleep. Really too old for dolls. But the "Toodles" were lifelike—for their jointed arms and legs could be positioned like a real baby in play—and I "had" to have one

of them, too. I named mine Dottie. Without talking or dancing or turning somersaults or clapping their hands, Dottie and her identical sister simply sat on our chair or lay on our beds. Their little hands and feet were placed in lifelike position by girls too old to pretend to be mothers, but not too old to love.

Truce in the Forest

Fritz Vincken

"It was Christmas Eve, and the last, desperate German offensive of World War II raged around our tiny cabin. Suddenly, there was a knock on the door . . ."

Many have written in, asking that this memorable Reader's Digest "First Person" Award story be included in this collection.

When we heard the knock on our door that Christmas Eve in 1944, neither Mother nor I had the slightest inkling of the quiet miracle that lay in store for us.

I was 12 then, and we were living in a small cottage in the Hürtgen Forest, near the German-Belgian border. Father had stayed at the cottage on hunting weekends before the war; when Allied bombers partly destroyed our hometown of Aachen, he sent us to live there. He had been ordered into the civil-defense fire guard in the border town on Monschau, four miles away.

"You'll be safe in the woods," he had told me. "Take care of Mother. Now you're the man of the family."

But, nine days before Christmas, Field Marshal von Rundstedt had launched the last, desperate German offensive of the war, and now, as I went to the door, the Battle of the Bulge was raging all around us. We heard the incessant booming of field guns; planes soared continuously overhead; at night, searchlights stabbed through the darkness. Thousands of Allied and German soldiers were fighting and dying nearby.

When that first knock came, Mother quickly blew out the candles; then, as I went to answer it, she stepped ahead of me and pushed open the door. Outside, like phantoms against the snowclad trees, stood two steel-helmeted men. One of them spoke to Mother in a language we did not understand, pointing to a third man lying in the snow. She realized before I did that these were American soldiers. *Enemies!*

Mother stood silent, motionless, her hand on my shoulder. They were armed and could have forced their entrance, yet they stood there and asked with their eyes. And the wounded man seemed more dead than alive. *"Kommt rein,"* Mother said finally. "Come in." The soldiers carried their comrade inside and stretched him out on my bed.

None of them understood German. Mother tried French, and one of the soldiers could converse in that language. As Mother went to look after the wounded man, she said to me, "The fingers of those two are numb. Take off their jackets and boots, and bring in a bucket of snow." Soon I was rubbing their blue feet with snow.

We learned that the stocky, dark-haired fellow was Jim; his friend, tall and slender, was Robin. Harry, the wounded one, was now sleeping on my bed, his face as white as the snow outside. They'd lost their battalion and had wandered in the forest for three days, looking for the Americans, hiding from the Germans. They hadn't shaved, but still, without their heavy coats, they looked merely like big boys. And that was the way Mother began to treat them.

Now Mother said to me, "Go get Hermann. And bring six potatoes."

This was a serious departure from our pre-Christmas plans. Hermann was the plump rooster (named after portly Hermann Göring, Hitler's No. 2, for whom Mother had little affection) that we had been fattening for weeks in the hope that Father would be home for Christmas. But, some hours before, when it was obvious that Father would not make it, Mother had decided that Hermann should live a few more days, in case Father could get home for New Year's. Now she had changed her mind again: Hermann would serve an immediate, pressing purpose.

While Jim and I helped with the cooking, Robin took care of Harry. He had a bullet through his upper leg, and had almost bled to death. Mother tore a bedsheet into long strips for bandages.

Soon, the tempting smell of roast chicken permeated our room. I was setting the table when once again there came a knock at the door. Expecting to find more lost Americans, I opened the door without hesitation. There stood four soldiers, wearing uniforms quite familiar to me after five years of war. They were *Wehrmacht*—Germans!

I was paralyzed with fear. Although still a child, I

knew the harsh law: sheltering enemy soldiers constituted high treason. We could all be shot! Mother was frightened, too. Her face was white, but she stepped outside and said, quietly, *Fröhliche Weihnachten.*" The soldiers wished her a Merry Christmas, too.

"We have lost our regiment and would like to wait for daylight," explained the corporal. "Can we rest here?"

"Of course," Mother replied, with a calmness born of panic. "You can also have a fine, warm meal and eat till the pot is empty."

The Germans smiled as they sniffed the aroma through the half-open door. "But," Mother added firmly, "we have three other guests, whom you may not consider friends." Now her voice was suddenly sterner than I'd ever heard it before. "This is Christmas Eve, and there will be no shooting here."

"Who's inside?" the corporal demanded. *"Amerikaner?"*

Mother looked at each frost-chilled face. "Listen," she said slowly. "You could be my sons, and so could those in there. A boy with a gunshot wound, fighting for his life. His two friends— lost like you and just as hungry and exhausted as you are. This one night," she turned to the corporal and raised her voice a little, "this Christmas night, let us forget about killing."

The corporal stared at her. There were two or three endless seconds of silence. Then Mother put an end to indecision. "Enough talking!" she ordered and clapped her hands sharply. "Please put your weapons here on the woodpile—and hurry up before the others eat the dinner!"

Dazedly, the four soldiers placed their arms on the pile of firewood just inside the door: three carbines, a light machine gun, and two bazookas. Meanwhile, Mother was speaking French rapidly to Jim. He said something in English, and to my amazement I saw the American boys, too, turn their weapons over to Mother.

Now, as Germans and Americans tensely rubbed elbows in the small room, Mother was really on her mettle. Never losing her smile, she tried to find a seat for everyone. We had only three chairs, but Mother's bed was big, and on it she placed two of the newcomers side by side with Jim and Robin.

Despite the strained atmosphere, Mother went right on preparing dinner. But Hermann wasn't going to grow any bigger, and now there were four more mouths to feed. "Quick," she whispered to me, "get more potatoes and some oats. These boys are hungry, and a starving man is an angry one."

While foraging in the storage room, I heard Harry moan. When I returned, one of the Germans had put on his glasses to inspect the American's wound. "Do you belong to the medical corps?" Mother asked him. "No," he answered. "But I studied medicine at Heidelberg until a few months ago." Thanks to the cold, he told the Americans in what sounded like fairly good English, Harry's wound hadn't become infected. "He is suffering from a severe loss of blood," he explained to Mother. "What he needs is rest and nourishment."

Relaxation was now beginning to replace suspicion. Even to me, all the soldiers looked very young as we sat there together. Heinz and Willi, both from Cologne, were 16. The German corporal, at 23, was the oldest of them all. From his food bag he drew out a bottle of red wine, and Heinz managed to find a loaf of rye bread. Mother cut that in small pieces to be served with the dinner; half the wine, however, she put away—"for the wounded boy."

Then Mother said grace. I noticed that there were tears in her eyes as she said the old, familiar words, *"Komm, Herr Jesus.* Be our guest." And as I looked around the table, I saw tears, too, in the eyes of the battle-weary soldiers, boys again, some from America, some from Germany, all far from home.

Just before midnight, Mother went to the doorstep and asked us to join her to look up at the Star of Bethlehem. We all stood beside her except Harry, who was sleeping. For all of us during that moment of silence, looking at the brightest star in the heavens, the war was a distant, almost-forgotten thing.

Our private armistice continued next morning. Harry woke in the early hours, and swallowed some broth that Mother fed him. With the dawn, it was apparent that he was becoming stronger. Mother now made him an invigorating drink from our one egg, the rest of the corporal's wine, and some sugar. Everyone else had oatmeal. Afterward, two poles and Mother's best tablecloth were fashioned into a stretcher for Harry.

The corporal then advised the Americans how to find their way back to their lines. Looking over Jim's map, the corporal pointed out a stream. "Continue along this creek," he said, "and you will find the 1st Army rebuilding its forces on its upper course." The medical student relayed the information in English.

"Why don't we head for Monschau?" Jim had the student ask. *"Nein!"* the corporal exclaimed. "We've retaken Monschau."

Now Mother gave them all back their weapons. "Be careful, boys," she said. "I want you to get home someday where you belong. God bless you all!" The German and American soldiers shook hands, and we watched them disappear in opposite directions.

When I returned inside, Mother had brought out the old family Bible. I glanced over her shoulder. The book was open to the Christmas story, the Birth in the Manger, and how the Wise Men came from afar bearing their gifts. Her finger was tracing the last line from Matthew 2:12: ". . . they departed into their own country another way."

A Full House

Madeleine L'Engle

It was Christmas . . . family time. And the Austin house was full: with a husband, a wife, four children, a grandfather, three dogs, and two cats. There was no more room—nevertheless, along came Evie, along came Eugenia, along came state troopers, along came Maria and Pepita.

Yet in spite of it . . . or because of it . . . it was a Christmas Eve to remember.

(Madeleine L'Engle [1918-   ] is recognized around the world as one of the finest writers of our time, having successfully published plays, poems, essays, autobiography, and fiction for both children and adults. Perhaps best known is her Time Fantasy Series *of children's books,* A Wrinkle in Time, A Wind in the Door, A Swiftly Tilting Planet, *and* Many Waters, *books that embody her unique blend of science fiction, family love, and moral responsibility.* A Wrinkle in Time *won the Newbery Medal in 1963, the Lewis Carroll Shelf Award in 1965, and was runner up for the Hans Christian Andersen Award in 1964. She also wrote a series of books based on her family, including* The Twenty-four Days Before Christmas: An Austin Family Story. *A practicing Christian, religion is crucial in all her writings.)*

To anybody who lives in a city or even a sizable town, it may not sound like much to be the director of a volunteer choir in a postcard church in a postcard village, but I was the choir director and largely responsible for the Christmas Eve service, so it was very much of a much for me. I settled my four children and my father, who was with us for Christmas, in a front pew and went up to the stuffy choir-robing room. I was missing my best baritone, my husband, Wally, because he had been called to the hospital. He's a country doctor, and I'm used to his pocket beeper going off during the church service. I missed him, of course, but I knew he'd been called to deliver a baby, and a Christmas baby is always a joy.

The service went beautifully. Nobody flatted, and Eugenia Underhill, my lead soprano, managed for once not to breathe in the middle of a word. The only near disaster came when she reached for the high C in "O Holy Night," hit it brilliantly—and then down fell her upper plate. Eugenia took it in good stride, pushed her teeth back in place and finished her solo. When she sat down, she doubled over with mirth.

The church looked lovely, lighted entirely by candlelight, with pine boughs and holly banking the windows. The Christmas Eve service is almost entirely music, hence my concern; there is never a sermon, but our minister reads excerpts from the Christmas sermons of John Donne and Martin Luther.

When the dismissal and blessings were over, I heaved a sigh of relief. Now I could attend to our own Christmas at home. I collected my family, and we went out into the night. A soft, feathery snow was beginning to fall. People called out "Goodnight" and "Merry Christmas." I was happily tired, and ready for some peace and quiet for the rest of the evening—our service is over by nine.

I hitched Rob, my sleeping youngest, from one hip to the other. The two girls, Vicky and Suzy, walked on either side of their grandfather; John, my eldest, was with me. They had all promised to go to bed without protest as soon as we had finished all our traditional Christmas rituals. We seem to add new ones each year so that Christmas Eve bedtime gets later and later.

I piled the kids into the station wagon, thrusting Rob into John's arms. Father and I got in the front, and I drove off into the snow, which was falling more heavily. I hoped that it would not be a blizzard and that Wally would get home before the roads got too bad.

Our house is on the crest of a hill, a mile out of the village. As I looked uphill, I could see the lights of our outdoor Christmas tree twinkling warmly through the snow. I turned up our back road, feeling suddenly very tired. When I drove up to the garage and saw that Wally's car was not there, I tried not to let Father or the children see my disappointment. I began ejecting the kids from the back. It was my father who first noticed what looked like a bundle of clothes by the storm door.

"Victoria," he called to me. "What's this?"

The bundle of clothes moved. A tear-stained face emerged, and I recognized Evie, who had moved from the village with her parents two years ago, when she was 16. She had been our favorite and most loyal baby-sitter, and we all missed her. I hadn't seen her—or heard anything about her—in all this time.

"Evie!" I cried. "What is it? What's the matter?"

She moved stiffly, as though she had been huddled there in the cold for a long time. Then she held her arms out to me in a childlike gesture. "Mrs. Austin—" She sighed as I bent down to kiss her. And then, "Mom threw me out. So I came here." She dropped the words simply, as though she had no doubt that she would find a welcome in our home. She had on a shapeless, inadequate coat, and a bare toe stuck through a hole in one of her sneakers.

I put my arms around her and helped her up. "Come in. You must be frozen."

The children were delighted to see Evie and crowded around, hugging her, so it was a few minutes before we got into the kitchen and past the dogs who were loudly welcoming us home. There were Mr. Rochester, our Great Dane; Colette, a silver-gray French poodle who bossed the big dog unmercifully; and, visiting us for the Christmas holidays while his owners were on vacation, a 10-month-old Manchester terrier named Guardian. Daffodil, our fluffy amber cat, jumped on top of the bridge to get out of the way, and Prune Whip, our black-and-white cat, skittered across the floor and into the living room.

The kids turned on lights all over downstairs, and John called, "Can I turn on the Christmas-tree lights?"

I turned again to Evie, who simply stood in the middle of the big kitchen-dining room, not moving. "Evie, welcome. I'm sorry it's such chaos—let me take your coat." At first she resisted and then let me slip the worn material off her shoulders. Under the coat she wore a sweater and a plaid skirt; the skirt did not button, but was fastened with a pin, and for an obvious reason: Evie was not about to produce another Christmas baby, but she was very definitely pregnant.

Her eyes followed mine. Rather defiantly, she said, "That's why I'm here."

I thought of Evie's indifferent parents, and I thought about Christmas Eve. I put my arm around her for a gentle hug. "Tell me about it."

"Do I have to?"

"I think it might help, Evie."

Suzy, 8 years old and still young enough to pull at my skirt and be whiny when she was tired, now did just that to get my full attention. "Let's put out the cookies and cocoa for Santa Claus *now*."

Suddenly there was an anguished shout from the living room. "Come quick!" John yelled, and I went running.

Guardian was sitting under the tree, a long piece of green ribbon hanging from his mouth. Around him was a pile of Christmas wrappings, all nicely chewed. While we were in church, our visiting dog had unwrapped almost every single package under the tree.

Vicky said, "But we won't know who anything came from . . ."

Suzy burst into tears. "That dog has ruined it all!"

Evie followed us in. She was carrying Rob, who was sleeping with his head down on her shoulder. Father looked at her with his special warm glance that took in and assessed any situation. "Sit down, Evie," he ordered.

I took Rob from her, and when she had more or less collapsed in Wally's special chair in front of the big fire-place, he asked, "When did you eat last?"

"I don't know. Yesterday, I think."

I dumped my sleeping child on the sofa and then headed for the kitchen, calling, "Vicky, Suzy, come help me make sandwiches. I'll warm up some soup. John, make up the couch in Daddy's office for Evie, please."

Our house is a typical square New England farm-house. Upstairs are four bedrooms. Downstairs we have a big, rambling kitchen-dining room, all unexpected angles and nooks; a large, L-shaped living room and my husband's office, which he uses two nights a week for his patients in the nearby village. As I took a big jar of vegetable soup from the refrigerator and poured a good helping into a saucepan, I could hear my father's and Evie's voices, low, quiet, and I wondered if Evie was pouring out her story to him. I remembered hearing that her father seldom came home without stopping first at the tavern and that her mother had the reputation of being no better than she should be. And yet I knew that their response to Evie's pregnancy would be one of righteous moral indignation. To my daughters I said, "There's some egg salad in the fridge. Make a big sandwich for Evie."

I lifted the curtains and looked out the window. The roads would soon be impassable. I wanted my husband to be with us, in the warmth and comfort of our home.

I went back to the stove and poured a bowl of soup for Evie. Vicky and Suzy had produced a messy but edible sandwich and then gone off. I called Evie, and she sat at the table and began to eat hungrily. I sat beside her. "How did it happen? Do I know him?"

She shook her head. "No. His name's Billy. After

we left here, I didn't feel—I didn't feel that anybody in the world loved me. I think that Mom and Pop are always happiest when I'm out of the house. When I was baby-sitting for you, I thought I saw what love was like. Mrs. Austin, I was lonely, I was so lonely it hurt. Then I met Billy, and I thought he loved me. So when he wanted to—I—but then I found out that it didn't have anything to do with love, at least not for Billy. When I got pregnant, he said, well, how did I even know it was his? Mrs. Austin, I never, never was with anyone else. When he said that, I know it was his way of telling me to get out, just like Mom and Pop."

The girls had wandered back into the kitchen while we were talking, and Suzy jogged at my elbow. "Why does Evie's tummy look so big?"

The phone rang. I called, "John, get it please."

In a moment he came into the kitchen, looking slightly baffled. "It was someone from the hospital saying Dad's on his way home, and would we please make up the bed in the waiting room."

Evie looked up from her soup. "Mrs. Austin—" she turned her frightened face toward me, fearful, no doubt, that we were going to put her out.

"It's all right, Evie." I was thinking quickly. "John, would you mind sleeping in the guest room with Grandfather?"

"If Grandfather doesn't mind."

My father called from the living room, "Grandfather would enjoy John's company."

"All right then, Evie." I poured more soup into her bowl. "You can sleep in John's bed. Rob will love sharing his room with you."

"But who is Daddy bringing home?" John asked.

"What's wrong with Evie's tummy?" Suzy persisted.

"And why didn't Daddy tell us?" Vicky asked.

"Tell us what?" Suzy demanded.

"Who he's bringing home with him!" John said.

Evie continued to spoon the soup into her mouth, at the same time struggling not to cry. I put one hand on her shoulder, and she reached up for it, asking softly, as the girls and John went into the living room, "Mrs. Austin, I knew you wouldn't turn me away on Christmas Eve, but what about . . . well, may I stay with you for a little while? I have some thinking to do."

"Of course you can, and you do have a lot of thinking to do—the future of your baby, for instance."

"I know. Now that it's getting so close, I'm beginning to get really scared. At first I thought I wanted the baby, I thought it would make Billy and me closer, make us a family like you and Dr. Austin and your kids, but now I know that was just wishful thinking. Sometimes I wish I could go back, be your baby-sitter again . . . Mrs. Austin, I just don't know what I'm going to do with a baby of my own."

I pressed her hand. "Evie, I know how you feel, but things have a way of working out. Try to stop worrying, at least tonight—it's Christmas Eve."

"And I'm home," Evie said. "I feel more at home in this house than anywhere else."

I thought of my own children and hoped that they would never have cause to say that about someone else's house. To Evie I said, "Relax then, and enjoy Christmas. The decisions don't have to be made tonight."

My father ambled into the kitchen, followed by the

three dogs. "I think the dogs are telling me they need to go out," he said. "I'll just walk around the house with them and see what the night is doing." He opened the kitchen door and let the dogs precede him.

I opened the curtains, not only to watch the progress of my father and the dogs, but to give myself a chance to think about Evie and how we could help her. More was needed, I knew, than just a few days' shelter. She had no money, no home, and a baby was on the way. . . . No wonder she looked scared—and trapped. I watched the falling snow and longed to hear the sound of my husband's car. Like Vicky, I wondered who on earth he was bringing home with him. Then I saw headlights coming up the road and heard a car slowing down, but the sound was not the slightly bronchial purr of Wally's car. Before I had a chance to wonder who it could be, the phone rang. "I'll get it!" Suzy yelled, and ran, beating Vicky. "Mother, it's Mrs. Underhill."

I went to the phone. Eugenia's voice came happily over the line. "Wasn't the Christmas Eve service beautiful! And did you see my teeth?" She laughed.

"You sang superbly, anyhow."

"Listen, why I called—and you have two ovens, don't you?"

"Yes."

"Something's happened to mine. The burners work, but the oven is dead, and there's no way I can get anyone to fix it now. So what I wondered is, can I cook my turkey in one of your ovens?"

"Sure," I said, though I'd expected to use the second oven for the creamed-onion casserole and sweet potatoes—but how could I say no to Eugenia?

"Can I come over with my turkey now?" she asked. "I like to put it in a slow oven Christmas Eve, the way you taught me. Then I won't have to bother you again tomorrow."

"Sure, Eugenia, come on over, but drive carefully."

"I will. Thanks," she said.

John murmured, "Just a typical Christmas Eve at the Austins," as the kitchen door opened, and my father and the dogs came bursting in, followed by a uniformed state trooper.

When Evie saw him, she looked scared.

My father introduced the trooper, who turned to me. "Mrs. Austin, I've been talking with your father here, and I think we've more or less sorted things out." Then he looked at Evie. "Young lady, we've been looking for you. We want to talk to you about your friends."

The color drained from her face.

"Don't be afraid," the trooper reassured her. "We just want to know where we can find you. I understand

that you'll be staying with the Austins for a while—for the next few weeks, at least." He looked at my father, who nodded, and I wondered what the two had said to each other. Was Evie in more trouble than I thought?

She murmured something inaudible, keeping her eyes fastened to her soup.

"Well, now, it's Christmas Eve," the trooper said, "and I'd like to be getting on home. It's bedtime for us all."

"We're waiting for Daddy," Suzy said. "He's on his way home."

"And he's bringing someone with him," Vicky added.

"Looks like you've got a full house," the trooper said. "Well, 'night, folks."

My father showed him out, then shut the door behind him.

"What was that—" John started to ask.

I quickly said, "What I want all of you to do is to go upstairs, right now, and get ready for bed. That's an order."

"But what about Daddy—"

"And whoever he's bringing —"

"And reading 'The Night Before Christmas' and Saint Luke—"

"And you haven't sung to us—"

I spoke through the clamor. "Upstairs. Now. You can come back down as soon as you're all ready for bed."

Evie rose. "Shall I get Rob?" I had the feeling she wanted to get away, escape my questions.

"We might as well leave him. Vicky, get Evie some nightclothes from my closet, please."

When they had all finally trooped upstairs, including Evie, I turned to my father who was perched on a stool by the kitchen counter. "All right, Dad, tell me about it," I said. "What did the officer tell you?"

"That soup smells mighty good," he said. I filled a bowl for him and waited.

Finally he said, "Evie was going with a bunch of kids who weren't much good. A couple of them were on drugs—not Evie, fortunately, or her boyfriend. And they stole some cars, just for kicks, and then abandoned them. The police are pretty sure that Evie wasn't involved, but they want to talk to her and her friends, and they've been trying to round them up. They went to her parents' house looking for her. Her mother and father made it seem as if she'd run away—they didn't mention that they'd put her out. All they did was denounce her, but they did suggest she might have come here."

"Poor Evie. There's so much good in her, and sometimes I wonder how, with her background. What did you tell the trooper?"

"I told him Evie was going to stay with you and Wally for the time being, that you would take responsibility for her. They still want to talk to her, but I convinced him to wait until after Christmas. I guess the trooper figured that, as long as she's with you, she would be looked after and out of harm's way."

"Thank goodness. All she needs is to be hauled into a station house on Christmas Eve—" Just then the heavy knocker on the kitchen door banged.

It was Eugenia, with a large turkey in a roasting pan in her arms. "I'll just pop it in the oven," she said. "If you think about basting it when you baste yours, OK, but it'll do all right by itself. Hey, you don't have yours in yet!"

What with one thing and another, I'd forgotten our turkey, but it was prepared and ready in the cold pantry. I whipped out and brought it in and put it in the other oven.

As Eugenia drove off, the dogs started with their welcoming bark, and I heard the sound of Wally's engine.

The children heard, too, and came rushing downstairs. "Wait!" I ordered. "Don't mob Daddy. And remember he has someone with him."

Evie came slowly downstairs, wrapped in an old blue plaid robe of mine. John opened the kitchen door, and the dogs went galloping out.

"Whoa! Down!" I could hear my husband command. And then, to the children, "Make way!" The children scattered, and Wally came in, his arm around a young woman whom I had never seen before. She was holding a baby in her arms.

"This is Maria Heraldo," Wally said. "Maria, my wife, Victoria. And—" He looked at the infant.

"Pepita," she said, "after her father."

Wally took the baby. "Take off your coat," he said to the mother. "Maria's husband was killed in an accident at work two weeks ago. Her family are all in South America, and she was due to be released from the hospital today. Christmas Eve didn't seem to me to be a very good time for her to be alone."

I looked at the baby, who had an amazing head of dark hair. "She isn't the baby—"

"That I delivered tonight? No, though that little boy was slow in coming—that's why we're so late." He smiled down at the young woman. "Pepita was born a week ago." He looked up and saw our children hovering in the doorway, Evie and my father behind them. When he saw Evie, he raised his eyebrows in a questioning gesture.

"Evie's going to be staying with us for a while," I told him. Explanations would come later. "Maria, would you like some soup?"

"I would," my husband said, "and Maria will have some, too." He glanced at the children. "Vicky and Suzy, will you go up to the attic, please, and bring down the cradle?"

They were off like a flash.

My husband questioned the young mother. "Tired?"

"No. I slept while the little boy was being delivered. So did Pepita." And she looked with radiant pride at her daughter who was sleeping again.

"Then let's all go into the living room and warm ourselves in front of the fire. We have some Christmas traditions you might like to share with us."

The young woman gazed up at him, at me, "I'm so grateful to you—"

"Nonsense. Come along."

Then Maria saw Evie, and I watched her eyes flick to Evie's belly, then upward, and the two young women exchanged a long look. Evie's glance shifted to the sleeping child, and then she held out her arms. Maria gently handed her the baby, and Evie took the child and cradled it in her arms. For the first time that evening a look of peace seemed to settle over her features.

It is not easy for a woman to raise a child alone, and Maria would probably go back to her family. In any case, her child had obviously been conceived in love, and even death could not take that away. Evie's eyes were full of tears as she carried Pepita into the living room, but she no longer looked so lost and afraid, and I had the feeling that whatever happened, Evie would be able to handle it. She would have our help—Wally's and mine— for as long as she needed it, but something told me that she wouldn't need it for long.

In a short while, Maria was ensconced in one of the big chairs, a bowl of soup on the table beside her. Evie put the baby in the cradle, and knelt, rocking it gently. Wally sat on the small sofa with Rob in his lap, a mug of soup in one hand. The two girls were curled up on the big davenport, one on either side of their grandfather, who had his arms around them. I sat across from Maria, and Evie came and sat on the footstool by me. John was on the floor in front of the fire. The only light was from the Christmas tree and the flickering flames of the fire. On the mantel were a cup of cocoa and a plate of cookies.

"Now," my husband said, "'Twas the night before Christmas, when all through the house . . .'"

When he had finished, with much applause from the children and Evie and Maria, he looked to me. "Your turn."

John jumped up and handed me my guitar. I played and sang, "I Wonder as I Wander," and then "In the Bleak Mid-winter," and ended up with "Let All Mortal Flesh Keep Silence." As I put the guitar away, I saw Maria reach out for Evie, and the two of them briefly clasped hands.

"And now," Wally said, "your turn, please, Grandfather."

My father opened his Bible and began to read. When he came to "And she brought forth her firstborn son, and wrapped him in swaddling clothes, and laid him in a manger; because there was no room for them in the inn," I looked at Maria, who was rocking the cradle with her foot while her baby murmured in her sleep. Evie, barely turning, keeping her eyes fastened on the sleeping infant, leaned her head against my knee, rubbing her cheek against the wool of my skirt.

Suzy was sleeping with her head down in her grandfather's lap, while he continued to read: "And suddenly there was with the angel a multitude of the heavenly host praising God, and saying, Glory to God in the highest, and on earth peace, good will toward men."

I remembered John saying, "Just a typical Christmas Eve at the Austins," and I wondered if there ever could be such a thing as a typical Christmas. For me, each one is unique. This year our house was blessed by Evie and her unborn child, by Eugenia's feeling free to come and put her turkey in our stove, and by Maria and Pepita turning our plain New England farmhouse into a stable.

Jolly Miss Enderby

Paul Gallico

Why is it that being overweight is equated with being jolly? How often might a smiling face hide a crying heart? Why don't we take the time to look behind the façade and search out the person behind?

"Jolly" Miss Enderby and those who supposedly knew her well were all of the above: yes, she was fat; yes, she was taken for granted; and yes, she was a most lonely woman . . . but having lost all hope that anyone would ever take the trouble to care.

(Paul Gallico [1897-1976], author of best sellers such as The Poseidon Adventure, The Snow Goose, Thomasina, The Lonely, *etc., often zeroed in on characters who were not what they seemed to be. This is one of his most disturbing—most disturbing because he hits most of us where we are weakest.)*

Jolly Miss Enderby! So she was known and spoken of, and who would have denied it seeing her round dimpled face alight with vivacity, her smile spreading to her extra chins, for she was a fat woman, as she sat at the piano in the classroom and played, sang, and conducted all at the same time.

Teacher of the second grade of the Dowsville Elementary School, the occasion was Miss Enderby's annual party and treat. Although the school had closed for the holidays the week before, her party always took place the afternoon of Christmas Eve and the class with parents came back for it. There were recitations, dancing, and singing. Afterward Miss Enderby served little cakes with colored icing and a choice of either cream soda or root beer. Miss Enderby paid for these herself.

Jolly Miss Enderby with the face of a cherub, her head, surrounded by an aureole of short cropped graying curls, nodding and one fat arm emerging from a flowered frock giving the tempo of the final carol. She beamed upon the children, the girls with great bows in their hair, the boys with scrubbed faces, the elders proud and stiff in their best clothing. Always cheerful, Miss Enderby made others cheerful too.

After that, the refreshments, and the children, urged by their mothers, shyly handing over their small, badly wrapped Christmas gifts that soon made a colorful pile upon Miss Enderby's desk.

One moment the classroom was still alive with the chattering of the group, congratulations, admonitions to the children to thank Miss Enderby, and the next it was empty and silent hard upon the last "Merry Christmas, Miss Enderby." It had not occurred to any of them to inquire how she would be spending her Christmas or perhaps to ask if she might like to join them at their Christmas dinner. And, of course, it did not occur to Miss Enderby either, that anyone should.

The teacher gently let down the lid of the old piano and went and sat at her desk to review the successful afternoon. The classroom, looking gay with its crisscrossing of scarlet and green crepe paper streamers, the pine branches plucked from the nearby woods, the holly and mistletoe, and its Christmas tree, was full of echoes and silences and things vividly remembered. Well past 50, unmarried, dedicated, Miss Enderby had been giving these parties for more than 20 years, and there were always endearing little incidents. This time it was Midge Thorgerson's wreath slipping down over her eyes during her solo dance and the Johnson boy forgetting his poem, bursting into tears, running to her and burying his face in her ample middle.

And the collection of gifts on her desk. Miss Enderby smiled at these. Then the echoes sounded no more, the memories began to fade, and there was only the empty classroom with the lowering winter sun momentarily setting the snow outside afire before it vanished. With all the human bodies no longer there the room was suddenly chilly, and Miss Enderby shivered slightly.

She rose and went about the business of tidying up, depositing the empty paper drinking cups into the big wire basket. She swept the dozen or so presents into her carryall along with a half-finished bottle of cream soda. When she walked down the corridor of the dark and deserted schoolhouse, her heel clicks sounded too loudly in her ears. She donned galoshes and the cloth coat that was never quite warm enough for their winters and went out into the frosty early evening, locking the door behind her.

As she turned homeward there was starshine overhead, and the colored lights of the Christmas trees outside people's houses glowed hospitably. Miss Enderby thought what a good community it was where folks put out Christmas trees so that everyone could enjoy them. She continued on to her lodgings in the boarding house of Mrs. Weedon at the far end of Chestnut Street. Mrs. Weedon did not have a Christmas tree on the front lawn.

Miss Enderby's quarters were at the back of the house. The bath was down the hall, but she had a basin in her room with a mirror from which a good deal of the silver backing had departed. She washed, put on lipstick very carefully, reordered her hair, and having completed the task, she said to the visible portion of her mirror image, "There you are, Miss Enderby," and went out again, this time to trudge down the six blocks to Greene's Cafeteria, where she took her meals.

The dingy restaurant had tried to greet Christmas with a few garlands, but it was jolly Miss Enderby who lit up the place when she came in and took her seat at the table in the rear by the kitchen door. The two waitresses, Bella and Madge, and the other patrons were always cheered by her presence.

Her slice of gray Yankee pot roast was concealed under a gluey brown sauce. While Miss Enderby wrestled with it Bella, a thin blond with untidy hair and a not too clean apron, had a lull and came over.

"Going to the movie tonight? It's Robert Redford and Paul Newman."

Miss Enderby shook her head and said, "No, I'm staying home and opening my presents."

"Presents?" repeated Bella. "Aren't you lucky."

Yes, I am, Miss Enderby thought to herself. Perhaps Bella wouldn't be getting any presents. "But you'll be coming in for the Turkey Dinner Christmas Special tomorrow, won't you? I seen the turkey. They're cooking it now."

"Of course," Miss Enderby replied. When she had finished she rose and said, "Goodnight, Bella. See you tomorrow."

Bella said with a slight smile of satisfaction, "I'm off tomorrow. Madge will be looking after you. I'm going to my sister's."

Miss Enderby's several chins outlined her pleased smile. "How nice for you, Bella." Miss Enderby had no living relations. But then neither did she have any envy nor self-pity. "Well then, I'll say 'Merry Christmas' now," and leaned over and kissed her.

The two waitresses watched her go out. Madge said to Bella, "Imagine having to eat Christmas dinner alone in a dump like this. It's different when you're working."

"Oh, she don't mind. She's always smiling," Bella replied.

Madge said "Uhuh" and walked away to a customer. Bella felt vaguely uncomfortable.

Back home in her room as Miss Enderby undid her parcels slowly so as to make them last longer she thought of Bella's words, "Aren't you lucky," and felt that indeed she was, for as the years of teaching came marching past in her mind, this last one could hold up its head, for it had been a good one. Each little packet on the table represented a child, and each child represented too a success or a failure, and there had been more successes than failures.

The first packet contained a cake of soap and its cheap scent suddenly overpowered the staleness of the furnishings of the room. From Kevin Hansen of the angel face and the dark heart; she had broken through to find the affection that also slumbered there. A string of 10-cent store beads. Anna Polanski; she really had improved. A colored wash cloth. Mary Cronin, one of her failures; Mary's head was empty. It would remain empty. She comforted herself with thinking, *You can't win them all.*

A self-propelling pencil, a bottle of cheap toilet water, a pincushion, a small badly made China cat, a decorated comb, a hand-embroidered doily, a box of homemade cookies.

The colorful discarded wrapping paper made her room gayer, and the tribute on the table before her filled jolly Miss Enderby's heart with gratitude, and in her mind's eye she saw them all once more as they had been that afternoon in their party clothes and heard again the noise and hubbub as they ate and drank their way through her treat. And then ere she knew it, the picture changed to herself sitting in the empty classroom and the little shiver that had come over her. Before she could prevent it, the shiver repeated itself there in her own room.

Never in a million years would Miss Enderby have admitted to herself that she was suddenly miserable and desperately lonely. She rose and went to the window that looked out upon Mrs. Weedon's untidy backyard. It had begun to snow again and she heard bells from the church. She turned away and suddenly tears began to fall from her eyes. Her stout heart fought against them valiantly. *Oh no no! Never admit that no one cared really.* She sat down at the table and regarded the small gifts, all there would ever be for her Christmas.

There came a timid knock at her door, and it opened slowly to admit Bella from Greene's Cafeteria. She stood there for a moment nonplussed by Miss Enderby's tears.

"Oh," she cried involuntarily, "Madge said you were always smiling."

"I was alone," said Miss Enderby. "There was no one to see me."

"Look," Bella said, "I got a favor to ask. My sister always says I can bring a friend. Christmas is a big party with her. Everyone is there. I . . . I . . . I never had a friend I could ask. Would you come, Miss Enderby, please?"

What healed Miss Enderby's great heart once more, dried her tears, and filled her with a great glow of love was the nobility of the little waitress who could so disguise the invitation, and the teacher's wonderful warm embracing smile broke forth again as she cried, "Oh Bella, I would love to. What a happy Christmas you will give me!"

On Christmas Day in the Morning

Grace Richmond

Guy was upset—well, more than upset. Of all the grown Fernald family (Oliver, Edson, Ralph, Guy, Carolyn, and Nan), only Guy had gone home for Christmas. And even he had merely popped in for a few hours.

Next Christmas, he argued, should be better. But convincing all five to leave spouses and children and sneak into the old house as if they were kids again—well that proved to be an uphill battle.

As for Guy, he didn't have a wife. And it was looking more and more like he never would.

(I found it several weeks ago in a St. George, Utah, antique store. On seeing it, I did a doubletake, then a tripletake, not believing my eyes. But there it was: undeniably a Christmas book by one of my all-time-favorite authors, Grace Richmond [1866-1959]. I was but a child when I first fell in love with her—and then the years have but deepened that attachment. I have savored her books, doling them out to read with the stinginess of a miser lest I complete her canon at too young an age. Her books are beloved still [by a small but discerning audience]; books such as The Second Violin, The Twenty-Fourth of June, Cherry Square, Foursquare, The Brown Study, Lights Up, At the South Gate, The Listening Post, Strawberry Acres, and the very popular Red Pepper books.

Since legendary Ladies Home Journal editor, Edward Bok was a devotee of hers, I had seen Richmond's books serialized, and even some of her stories featured in old magazines—but never until this day, a Christmas story. I would have paid almost anything the proprietor asked for it—I just knew it would be good!

It was . . . and is. Actually, the book features two related stories about the same family, "On Christmas Day in the Morning" and a second [almost twice as long], "On Christmas Day in the Evening"—two of the finest things she ever wrote.

In fact, no archeologist could possibly be more excited over his find than I. So much so that I bumped one of the stories in this book in order to make room for "On Christmas Day in the Morning.")

* * * * *

And all the angels in heaven do sing,
On Christmas Day, on Christmas Day;
And all the bells on earth do ring,
On Christmas Day in the morning.
                    —Old Song.

That Christmas Day virtually began a whole year beforehand, with a red-hot letter written by Guy Fernald to his younger sister, Nan, who had been married to Samuel Burnett just two-and-one-half years. The letter was read aloud by Mrs. Burnett to her husband at the breakfast table, the second day after Christmas. From start to finish it was upon one subject, and it read as follows:

Dear Nan:

It's a confounded, full-grown shame that not a soul of us all got home for Christmas—except yours truly, and he only for a couple of hours. What have the blessed old folks done to us that we treat them like this? I was invited to the Sewalls' for the day, and went, of course—you know why. We had a ripping time, but along toward evening I began to feel worried. I really thought Ralph was home—he wrote me that he might swing round that way by the holidays—but I knew the rest of you were all wrapped up in your own Christmas trees and weren't going to get there.

Well, I took the seven-thirty down and walked in on them. Sitting all alone by the fire, by George, just like the pictures you see of "The Birds All Flown," and that sort of thing. I felt gulpish in my throat, on my honour I did, when I looked at them. Mother just gave one gasp and flew into my arms, and Dad got up more slowly—his rheumatism is worse than ever this winter—and came over and I thought he'd shake my hand off. Well—I sat down between them by the fire, and pretty soon I got down in the old way on a cushion by Mother, and let her run her fingers through my hair, the way she used to—and Nan, I'll be indicted for perjury if her hand wasn't trembly. They were so glad to see me it made my throat ache.

Ralph had written he couldn't get round, and of course you'd all written and sent them things—jolly things, and they appreciated them. But—blame it all—they were just dead lonesome—and the whole outfit of us within 300 miles, most within 30!

Nan—next Christmas it's going to be different. That's all I say. I've got it all planned out. The idea popped into my head when I came away last night. Not that they had a word of blame—not they. They understood all about the children, and the cold snap, and Ed's being under the weather, and Oliver's wife's neuralgia, and Ralph's girl in the West, and all that. But that didn't make the thing any easier for them. As I say, next year—but you'll all hear from me then. Meanwhile—run down and see them once or twice this winter, will you, Nan? Somehow it struck me they aren't so young as—they used to be.

Splendid winter weather. Margaret Sewall's a peach, but I don't seem to make much headway. My best to Sam.

Your affectionate brother,
Guy.

Sunny Nan had felt a slight choking in her own throat as she read this letter. "We really must make an effort to be there Christmas next year, Sam," she said to her husband, and Sam assented cheerfully. He only wished there were a father and mother somewhere in the world for him to go home to.

Guy wrote the same sort of thing, with more or less detail, to Edson and Oliver, his married elder brothers; to Ralph, his unmarried brother; and to Carolyn—Mrs. Charles Wetmore, his other—and elder—married sister. He received varied and more or less sympathetic responses, to the effect that with so many little children, and such snowdrifts as always blocked the roads leading toward North Estabrook, it really was not strange—and of course somebody would go next year. But they had all sent the nicest gifts they could find. Didn't Guy think Mother liked those beautiful Russian sables Ralph sent her? And wasn't Father pleased with his gold-headed cane from Oliver? Surely with such presents pouring in from all the children, Father and Mother Fernald couldn't feel so awfully neglected!

"Gold-headed cane be hanged!" Guy exploded when he read this last sentence from the letter of Marian, Oliver's wife. "I'll bet she put him up to it. If anybody dares give me a gold-headed cane before I'm 95 I'll thrash him with it on the spot. He wasn't using it, either—bless him. He had his old hickory stick, and he wouldn't have had that if that abominable rheumatism hadn't gripped him so hard. He isn't old enough to use a cane, by jolly, and Ol ought to know it, if Marian doesn't. I'm glad I sent him that typewriter. He liked that, I know he did, and it'll amuse him, too—not make

him think he's ready to die!"

Guy was not the fellow to forget anything which had taken hold of him as that pathetic Christmas homecoming had done. When the year had nearly rolled around, the first of December saw him at work getting his plans in train. He began with his eldest brother, Oliver, because he considered Mrs. Oliver the hardest proposition he had to tackle in the carrying out of his idea.

"You see," he expounded patiently, as they sat and stared at him, "it isn't that they aren't always awfully glad to see the whole outfit, children and all, but it just struck me it would do 'em a lot of good to revive old times. I thought if we could make it just as much as possible like one of the old Christmases before anybody got married—hang up the stockings and all, you know—it would give them a mighty jolly surprise. I plan to have us all creep in in the night and go to bed in our old rooms. And then in the morning— See?"

Mrs. Oliver looked at him. An eager flush lit his still boyish face—Guy was 28—and his blue eyes were very bright. His lithe, muscular figure bent toward her pleadingly; all his arguments were aimed at her. Oliver sat back in his impassive way and watched them both. It could not be denied that it was Marian's decisions which usually ruled in matters of this sort.

"It seems to me a very strange plan," was Mrs. Oliver's comment, when Guy had laid the whole thing before her in the most tactful manner he could command. She spoke rather coldly. "It is not usual to think that families should be broken up like this on Christmas Day, of all days in the year. Four families, with somebody gone—a mother or a father—just to please two elderly people who expect nothing of the sort, and who understand just why we can't all get home at once. Don't you think you are really asking a good deal?"

Guy kept his temper, though it was hard work. "It doesn't seem to me I am," he answered quite gently. "It's only for once. I really don't think Father and Mother would care much what sort of presents we brought them, if we only came ourselves. Of course, I know I'm asking a sacrifice of each family, and it may seem almost an insult not to invite the children and all, yet—perhaps next year we'll try a gathering of all the clans. But just for this year—honestly—I do awfully wish you'd give me my way. If you'd seen those two last Christmas—"

He broke off, glancing appealingly at Oliver himself. To his surprise, that gentleman shifted his pipe to the corner of his mouth and put a few pertinent questions to his younger brother. Had he thought it all out? What time should they arrive there? How early on the day after Christmas could they get away? Was he positive they could all crowd into the house without rousing and alarming the pair?

"Sure thing," Guy declared, quickly. "Marietta—well, you know I've had the soft side of her old heart ever since I was born, somehow. I talked it all over with her last year, and I'm solid with her, all right. She'll work the game. You see, Father's quite a bit deaf now—"

"Father deaf?"

"Sure. Didn't you know it?"

"Forgotten. But Mother'd hear us."

"No, she wouldn't. Don't you know how she trusts everything about the house to Marietta since she got that fall—"

"Mother get a fall?"

"Why, yes!" Guy stared at his brother with some impatience. "Don't you remember she fell down the back stairs a year ago last October, and hurt her knee?"

"Certainly, Oliver," his wife interposed. "I wrote for you to tell her how sorry we were. But I supposed she had entirely recovered."

"She's a little bit lame, and always will be," said Guy, a touch of reproach in his tone. "Her knee stiffens up in the night, and she doesn't get up and go prowling about at the least noise, the way she used to. Marietta won't let her. So if we make a whisper of noise Marietta'll tell her it's the cat or something. No question at all!—it can be worked all right. The only thing that worries me is the fear that I can't get you all to take hold of the scheme. On my word, Ol"—he turned quite away from his sister-in-law's critical gaze and faced his brother with something like indignation in his frank young eyes—"don't we owe the old home anything but a present tied up in tissue paper once a year?"

Marian began to speak. She thought Guy was exceeding his rights in talking as if they had been at fault. It was not often that elderly people had so many children within call—loyal children who would do anything within reason. But certainly a man owed something to his own family. And at Christmas! Why not carry out this plan at some other—

Her husband abruptly interrupted her. He took his pipe quite out of his mouth and spoke decidedly.

"Guy, I believe you're right. I'll be sorry to desert

my own kids, of course, but I rather think they can stand it for once. If the others fall into line, you may count on me."

Guy got away, feeling that the worst of his troubles was over. In his younger sister, Nan, he hoped to find an ardent ally and he was not disappointed. Carolyn—Mrs. Charles Wetmore—also fell in heartily with the plan. Ralph, from somewhere in the far West, wrote that he would get home or break a leg. Edson thought the idea rather a foolish one, but was persuaded by Jessica, his wife—whom Guy privately declared a trump—that he must go by all means. And so they all fell into line, and there remained for Guy only the working out of the details.

"Mis' Fernald"—Marietta Cooley strove with all the decision of which she was capable to keep her high-pitched, middle-aged voice in order—"'fore you get to bed I'm most forgettin' what I was to ask you. I s'pose you'll laugh, but Guy—he wrote me partic'lar he wanted you and his father to"—Marietta's rather stern, thin face took on a curious expression—"to hang up your stockin's."

Mrs. Fernald paused in the doorway of the bedroom opening from the sitting-room downstairs. She looked back at Marietta with her gentle smile.

"Guy wrote that?" she asked. "Then—it almost looks as if he might be coming himself, doesn't it, Marietta?"

"Well, I don't know's I'd really expect him," Marietta replied, turning her face away and busying herself about the hearth. "I guess what he meant was more in the way of a surprise for a Christmas present—something that'll go into a stockin', maybe."

"It's rather odd he should have written you to ask me," mused Mrs. Fernald, as she looked for the stockings.

Marietta considered rapidly. "Well, I s'pose he intended for me to get 'em on the sly without mentionin' it to you, an' put in what he sent, but I sort of guessed you might like to fall in with his idee by hangin' 'em up yourself, here by the chimbley, where the children all used to do it. Here's the nails, same as they always was."

Mrs. Fernald found the stockings, and touched her husband on the shoulder, as he sat unlacing his shoes. "Father, Guy wrote he wanted us to hang up our stockings," she said, raising her voice a little and speaking very distinctly. The elderly man beside her looked up, smiling.

"Well, well," he said, "anything to please the boy. It doesn't seem more than a year since he was a little fellow hanging up his own stocking, does it, Mother?"

The stockings were hung in silence. They looked thin and lonely as they dangled beside the dying fire. Marietta hastened to make them less lonely. "Well," she said, in a shame-faced way, "the silly boy said I was to hang mine, too. Goodness knows what he'll find to put into it that'll fit, 'less it's a poker."

They smiled kindly at her, wished her good night, and went back into their own room. The little episode had aroused no suspicions. It was very like Guy's affectionate boyishness.

"I presume he'll be down," said Mrs. Fernald, as she limped quietly about the room, making ready for bed. "Don't you remember how he surprised us last year? I'm sorry the others can't come. Of course, I sent them all the invitation, just as usual—I shall always do that—but it is pretty snowy weather, and I suppose they don't quite like to risk it."

Presently, as she was putting out the light, she heard Marietta at the door.

"Mis' Fernald, Peter Piper's got back in this part o' the house, somehow, and I can't lay hands on him. Beats me how cute that cat is. Seem's if he knows when I'm goin' to put him out in the woodshed. I don't think likely he'll do no harm, but I thought I'd tell you, so 'f you heard any queer noises in the night you'd know it was Peter."

"Very well, Marietta"—the soft voice came back to the schemer on the other side of the door. "Peter will be all right, wherever he is. I shan't be alarmed if I hear him."

"All right, Mis' Fernald; I just thought I'd let you know," and the guileful one went grinning away.

There was a long silence in the quiet sleeping-room. Then, out of the darkness, came this little colloquy:

"Emeline, you aren't getting to sleep."

"I—know I'm not, John. I—Christmas Eve keeps one awake, somehow. It always did."

"Yes. . . . I don't suppose the children realize at all, do they?"

"Oh, no—oh, no! They don't realize—they never will, till—they're here themselves. It's all right. I think—I think at least Guy will be down tomorrow, don't you?"

"I guess maybe he will." Then, after a short silence. "Mother—you've got me, you know. You know—you've always got me, dear."

"Yes." She would not let him hear the sob in her voice. She crept close, and spoke cheerfully in his best ear. "And you've got me, Johnny Boy!"

"Thank the Lord, I have!"

So, counting their blessings, they fell asleep at last. But, even in sleep, one set of lashes was strangely wet.

"My goodness, what a drift!"

"Lucky we weren't two hours later."

"Sh-h—they might hear us."

"Nan, stop laughing, or I'll drop a snowball down your neck!"

"Here, Carol, give me your hand. I'll plough you through. Large bodies move slowly, of course, but go elbows first and you'll get there."

"Can't you get that door open? I'll bet it's frozen fast."

A light showed inside the kitchen. The storm door swung open, propelled by force from inside. A cautious voice said low: "That the Fernald family?"

A chorus of whispers came back at Miss Marietta Cooley:

"Yes, yes—let us in, we're freezing."

"You bet we're the Fernald family—every man-Jack of us—not one missing."

"Oh, Marietta—you dear old thing!"

"Hurry up—this is their side of the house."

"Sh-h-h—"

"Carol, your sh-h-ishes would wake the dead!"

Stumbling over their own feet and bundles in the endeavor to be preternaturally quiet, the crew poured into the warm kitchen. Bearded Oliver, oldest of the clan; stout Edson, big Ralph, tall and slender Guy—and the two daughters of the house, Carolyn, growing plump and rosy at 30; Nan, slim and girlish at 24—they were all there. Marietta heaved a sigh of content as she looked them over.

"Well, I didn't really think you'd get here—all of you. Thank the Lord you have. I s'pose you're tearin' hungry, bein' past 'leven. If you think you can eat quiet as cats, I'll feed you, but if you're goin' to make as much rumpus as you did comin' round the corner o' the woodshed I'll have to pack you straight off to bed up the back stairs."

They pleaded for mercy and hot food. They got it—everything that could be had that would diffuse no odour of cookery through the house. Smoking clam-broth, a great pot of baked beans, cold meats, and jellies—they had no reason to complain of their reception. They ate hungrily with the appetites of winter travel.

"Say, but this is great," exulted Ralph, the stalwart, consuming a huge wedge of mince pie with a fine disregard for any consequences that might overtake him. "This alone is worth it. I haven't eaten such pie in a century. What a jolly place this old kitchen is! Let's have a candy-pull tomorrow. I haven't been home Christmas in—let me see—I believe it's six—seven—yes, seven years. Look here: there's been some excuse for me, but what about you people that live near?"

He looked accusingly about. Carolyn got up and came around to him. "Don't talk about it tonight," she whispered. "We haven't any of us realized how long it's been."

"We'll get off to bed now," Guy declared, rising. "I can't get over the feeling that they may catch us down here. If either of them should want some hot water or anything—"

"The dining room door's bolted," Marietta assured him, "but it might need explainin' if I had to bring 'em hot water by way of the parlour. Now, go awful careful up them stairs. They're pretty near over your ma's head, but I don't dare have you tramp through the sittin'-room to the front ones. Now, remember that seventh stair creaks like Ned—you've got to step right on the outside edge of it to keep it quiet. I don't know but what you boys better step right up over that seventh stair without touchin' foot to it."

"All right—we'll step!"

"Who's going to fix the bundles?" Carolyn paused to ask as she started up the stairs.

"Marietta," Guy answered. "I've labeled every one, so it'll be easy. If they hear paper rattle, they'll think it's the usual presents we've sent on, and if they come out they'll see Marietta, so it's all right. Quiet, now. Remember the seventh stair!"

They crept up, one by one, each to his or her old room. There needed to be no "doubling up," for the house was large, and each room had been left precisely as its owner had left it. It was rather ghostly, this stealing silently about with candles, and in the necessity for the suppression of speech the animation of the party rather suffered eclipse. It was late, and they were beginning to be sleepy, so they were soon in bed. But, somehow, once composed for slumber, more than one grew wakeful again.

Guy, lying staring at a patch of wintry moonlight on the odd striped paper of his wall—it had stopped snowing since they had come into the house, and the clouds had broken away, leaving a brilliant sky—discovered his door to be softly opening. The glimmer of a candle filtered through the crack, a voice whispered his name.

"Who is it?" he answered under his breath.

"It's Nan. May I come in?"

"Of course. What's up?"

"Nothing. I wanted to talk a minute." She came

noiselessly in, wrapped in a woolly scarlet kimono, scarlet slippers on her feet, her brown braids hanging down her back. The frost-bloom lately on her cheeks had melted into a ruddy glow, her eyes were stars. She set her candle on the little stand, and she sat on the edge of Guy's bed. He raised himself on his elbow and lay looking appreciatively at her.

"This is like old times," he said. "But won't you be cold?"

"Not a bit. I'm only going to stay a minute. Anyhow, this thing is warm as toast. . . . Yes, isn't it like old times?"

"Got your lessons for tomorrow?"

She laughed. "All but my Caesar. You'll help me with that, in the morning, won't you?"

"Sure—if you'll make some cushions for my bobs."

"I will. Guy—how's Lucy Harper?"

"She's all right. How's Bob Fields?"

"Oh, I don't care for him, now!" She tossed her head.

He kept up the play. "Like Dave Strong better, huh? He's a softy."

"He isn't. Oh, Guy—I heard you had a new girl."

"New girl nothing. Don't care for girls."

"Yes, you do. At least I think you do. Her name's—Margaret."

The play ceased abruptly. Guy's face changed. "Perhaps I do," he murmured, while his sister watched him in the candlelight.

"She won't answer yet?" she asked very gently.

"Not a word."

"You've cared a good while, haven't you, dear?"

"Seems like ages. Suppose it isn't."

"No—only two years, really caring hard. Plenty of time left."

He moved his head impatiently. "Yes, if I didn't mind seeing her smile on Tommy Gower—de'il take him—just as sweetly as she smiles on me. If she ever held out the tip of her finger to me, I'd seize it and hold onto it for fair. But she doesn't. She won't. And she's going south next week for the rest of the winter, and there's a fellow down there in South Carolina where she goes—oh, he—he's red-headed after her, like the rest of us. And, well—I'm up against it good and hard, Nan, and that's the truth."

"Poor boy. And you gave up going to see her on Christmas Day, and came down here into the country just to—"

"Just to get even with myself for the way I've neglected 'em these two years while my head's been so full of—her. It isn't fair. After last year I'd have come home today if it had meant I had to lose—well—Margaret knows I'm here. I don't know what she thinks."

"I don't believe, Guy, boy, she thinks the less of you. Yes—I must go. It will all come right in the end, dear—I'm sure of it. No, I don't know how Margaret feels. Goodnight—goodnight!"

Christmas morning, breaking upon a wintry world—the star in the east long set. Outside the house a great silence of drift-wrapped hill and plain; inside, a crackling fire upon a wide hearth, and a pair of elderly people waking to a lonely holiday.

Mrs. Fernald crept to the door of her room—the injured knee always made walking difficult after a night's quiet. She meant to sit down by the fire which she had lately heard Marietta stirring and feeding into activity, and warm herself at its flame. She remembered with a sad little smile that she and John had hung their stockings there, and looked to see what miracle had been wrought in the night.

"*Father!*" Her voice caught in her throat. . . . What was all this? . . . By some mysterious influence her husband learned that she was calling him, though he had not really heard. He came to the door and looked at her, then at the chimneypiece where the stockings hung—a long row of them, as they had not hung since the children grew up—stockings of quality: one of brown silk, Nan's; a fine gray sock with scarlet clocks, Ralph's—all stuffed to the top, with bundles overflowing upon the chimneypiece and even to the floor below.

"What's this—what's this?" John Fernald's voice was puzzled. "Whose are these?" He limped closer. He put on his spectacles and stared hard at a parcel protruding from the sock with the scarlet clocks.

"'*Merry Christmas to Ralph from Nan,*'" he read. "'To Ralph from Nan,'" he repeated vaguely. His gaze turned to his wife. His eyes were wide like a child's. But she was getting to her feet, from the chair into which she had dropped.

"The children!" she was saying. "They—they—John—they must be *here!*"

He followed her through the chilly hall to the front staircase, seldom used now, and up—as rapidly as those slow, stiff joints would allow. Trembling, Mrs. Fernald pushed open the first door at the top.

A rumpled brown head raised itself from among the pillows, a pair of sleepy but affectionate brown eyes smiled back at the two faces peering in, and a voice brimful of mirth cried softly: "Merry Christmas, Mammy and Daddy!" They stared at her, their eyes growing misty. *It was their little daughter Nan, not yet grown up!*

They could not believe it. Even when they had been to every room—had seen their big son Ralph, still sleeping, his yet youthful face, full of healthy colour, pillowed on his brawny arm, and his mother had gently kissed him awake to be half-strangled in his hug—when they had met Edson's hearty laugh as he fired a pillow at them—carefully, so that his father could catch it; when they had seen plump pretty Carol pulling on her stockings as she sat on the floor smiling up at them; Oliver, advancing to meet them in his bath-robe and slippers; Guy, holding out both arms from above his blankets, and shouting "Merry Christmas! And how do you like your children?"—even then it was difficult to realize that not one was missing—and that no one else was there. Unconsciously Mrs. Fernald found herself looking about for the sons' wives and daughters' husbands and children. She loved them all—yet—to have her own, and no others, just for this one day—it was happiness indeed.

When they were all downstairs, about the fire, there was great rejoicing. They had Marietta in; indeed, she had been hovering continuously in the background, to the apparently frightful jeopardy of the breakfast in preparation, upon which, nevertheless, she had managed to keep a practiced eye.

"And you were in on it, Marietta?" Mr. Fernald said to her in astonishment, when he first saw her. "How in the world did you get all these people into the house and to bed without waking us?"

"It was pretty consid'able of a risk," Marietta replied, with modest pride, "seein' as how they was inclined to be middlin' lively. But I kep' a-hushin' 'em up, and I filled 'em up so full of victuals they couldn't talk. I didn't know's there'd be any eatables left for today," she added—which last remark, since she had been slyly baking for a week, Guy thought might be considered pure bluff.

At the breakfast table, while the eight heads were bent, this thanksgiving arose, as the master of the house, in a voice not quite steady, offered it to One Unseen:

Thou who camest to us on that first Christmas Day, we bless Thee for this good and perfect gift Thou sendest us today, that Thou forgettest us not in these later years, but givest us the greatest joy of our lives in these our loyal children.

Nan's hand clutched Guy's under the table. "Doesn't that make it worth it?" his grasp said to her, and hers replied with a frantic pressure, "Indeed it does, but we don't deserve it."

. . . It was late in the afternoon, a tremendous Christmas dinner well over, and the group scattered, when Guy and his mother sat alone by the fire. The "boys" had gone out to the great stock barn with their father to talk over with him every detail of the prosperous business he, with the help of an invaluable assistant, was yet able to manage. Carolyn and Nan had ostensibly gone with them, but in reality the former was calling upon an old friend of her childhood, and the latter had begged a horse and sleigh and driven merrily away alone upon an errand she would tell no one but her mother.

Mrs. Fernald sat in her low chair at the side of the hearth, her son upon a cushion at her feet, his head resting against her knee. Her slender fingers were gently threading the thick locks of his hair, as she listened while he talked to her of everything in his life, and, at last, of the one thing he cared most about.

"Sometimes I get desperate and think I may as well give her up for good and all," he was saying. "She's so—so—*elusive*—I don't know any other word for it. I never can tell how I stand with her. She's going south next week. I've asked her to answer me before she goes. Somehow I've clung to the hope that I'd get my answer today. You'll laugh, but I left word with my office boy to wire me if a note or anything from her came. It's four o'clock, and I haven't heard. She—you see, I can't help thinking it's because she's going to—turn me down—and—hates to do it—Christmas Day!"

He turned suddenly and buried his face in his mother's lap; his shoulders heaved a little in spite of himself. His mother's hand caressed his head more tenderly than ever, but, if he could have seen, her eyes were very bright.

They were silent for a long time. Then suddenly a jingle of sleigh bells approached through the falling winter twilight, drew near, and stopped at the door. Guy's mother laid her hands upon his shoulders. "Son," she said, "there's someone stopping now. Perhaps it's the boy with a message from the station."

He was on his feet in an instant. Her eyes followed him as he rushed away through the hall. Then she rose and quietly closed the sitting-room door behind him.

As Guy flung open the front door, a tall and slender figure in gray furs and a wide gray hat was coming up the walk. Eyes whose glance had long been his dearest torture met Guy Fernald's and fell. Lips like which there were no others in the world smiled tremulously in response to his eager exclamation. And over the piquant young face rose an exquisite color that was not altogether born of the wintry air. The girl who for two years had been only "elusive" had taken the significant step of coming to North Estabrook in response to an eloquent telephone message sent that morning by Nan.

Holding both her hands fast, Guy led her up into the house—and found himself alone with her in the shadowy hall. With one gay shout Nan had driven away toward the barn. The inner doors were all closed. Blessing the wondrous sagacity of his womankind, Guy took advantage of his moment.

"Nan brought you—I see that. I know you're very fond of her, but—you didn't come wholly to please her, did you—Margaret?"

"Not wholly."

"I've been looking all day for my answer. I—oh—I wonder if—" he was gathering courage from her aspect, which for the first time in his experience failed to keep him at a distance—"*dare I think you—bring it?*"

She slowly lifted her face. "I thought it was so—so dear of you," she murmured, "to come home to your people instead of—staying with me. I thought you deserved—what you say—you want—"

"*Margaret—you—*"

"I haven't given you any Christmas present. Will—I—do?"

"Will *you* do! . . . Oh!" It was a great explosive sigh of relief and joy, and as he gave vent to it he caught her close. "Will—you—do? . . . Will—you—*do*! . . . I rather *think you will!*"

"Emeline—"

"Yes, John dear?"

"You're not—crying?"

OH, no—no, no, John!" *What a blessing deafness is sometimes! The ear cannot detect the delicate tremolo that might tell the story too plainly. And in the darkness of night, the eye cannot see.*

"It's been a pretty nice day, hasn't it?"

"A beautiful day!"

"I guess there's no doubt but the children care a good deal for the old folks yet."

"No doubt at all, dear."

"It's good to think they're all asleep under the roof once more, isn't it?—And one extra one. We like her, don't we?"

"Oh, very, very much!"

"Yes, Guy's done well. I always thought he'd get her, if he hung on. The Fernalds always hang on, but Guy's got a mite of a temper—I didn't know but he might let go a little too soon. Well—it's great to think they all plan to spend every Christmas Day with us, isn't it, Emeline?"

"Yes, dear—it's great."

"Well—I must let you go to sleep. It's been a big day, and I guess you're tired. Emeline, we've not only got each other—we've got the children too. That's a pretty happy thing at our age, isn't it, now?"

"Yes—yes."

"Goodnight—Christmas Night, Emeline."

"Goodnight, dear."

Roses in December

Sybil Haddock

Jabez was self-sufficient: he needed no one and didn't wish to be needed by anyone. He was crusty and seemingly devoid of sentiment and warmth.

Then somebody began sending out gifts under his signature—and his doorbell started ringing.

This very old Canadian story had almost vanished from memory. How good it feels to restore its life!

Jabez Oldbury was stepping across the hall of his comfortable home on his way to the conservatory. He paused and listened. From the kitchen came the sound of a voice singing:

"From the eastern mountains,
  Pressing on they come,
  Wise men in their wisdom,
  To His humble home."

Jabez had no ear for music, but that fact did not account for the deep frown he wore between his eyebrows.

He disliked Christmas, and he hated to be reminded of the festive season. The words of the Christmas hymn made him feel as one supposes a cat feels when its fur stands on end at the sight of a dog.

There was something about Christmas that always made Jabez feel like that, and he never failed to remark that he was thankful when it was over.

People did such idiotic things that they would never dream of doing at any other time. They gave without discrimination; they helped people without first finding out whether they deserved help; folk were foolish and sentimental at Christmas. Jabez was never sentimental, and he never gave anything away unless he was sure of getting its equivalent back again—or more. To his wealthy friends who were in need of nothing he gave expensive gifts. If he knew he would only get a card, he sent a card. It had never occurred to him to distribute his gifts in any other way, and somehow he never got out of Christmas what other people seemed to get.

It simply made him feel more irritable than usual, and he wished his housekeeper would not sing about it. At the same time it was impossible for him to ask her not to sing about Christmas, for Mrs. Simpson was worth her weight in gold to Jabez, and he knew it.

His house was perfectly kept, and as far as it was possible with a man like Jabez for its master, Mrs. Simpson had made it a home as well as a house.

The frown Jabez was wearing grew deeper, as he realized that he must put up with the singing, much as he disliked it. He turned to continue his journey to the conservatory, when through the opaque glass in the front door he saw something. It was somebody lifting a hand to ring the bell. Jabez strode to the door and flung it open.

On the step stood a woman whom he had often seen in the village a mile from his house. Her shabby clothes were not of recent fashion, and she breathed heavily, as though she had been running.

Jabez wondered snobbishly what she was doing at his front door, surely the tradesman's entrance was the place for her. That thought flashed through his mind, and then vanished. It was banished by something more amazing.

Jabez forgot everything except the expression in the eyes of the woman who was looking at him. Never in his 50 years had any person looked at him in the same way. Jabez could not define the strange feeling it gave him, but in a subconscious way he knew that he liked it. For a moment they stared at one another. Jabez amazed, the woman breathless. Then, "Oh, sir," she gasped, "I couldn't rest till I'd thanked you."

"Thanked me!" exclaimed Jabez, "what—"

"The money'll set my boy up, sir, and—and—"

"My good woman," Jabez began, and then, to his great discomfort, his amazing visitor burst into tears. Whilst her face worked with emotion she could not control, she seized his hand, shook it as it had never been shaken before, pushed her hat more firmly on to her head, and rushed away. Jabez stood there, by his own front door, looking utterly foolish, too astonished to do anything but open and close his mouth like a fish out of water.

He had not the faintest idea what the woman had been talking about.

114

He smoothed the place on his head where he should have had hair, straightened his tie, patted his coat, and turned toward the kitchen from whence came that irritating singing. He opened the kitchen door.

"Mrs. Simpson," he said, "do you know a Mrs. Trim who lives in the village!"

Mrs. Simpson looked up from a sheet she was mending. It dawned on Jabez for the first time she hardly looked like a housekeeper. One associated such a lady with black clothes and prim and proper air. Mrs. Simpson wore neither. Her gray skirt and pullover were becoming to her snow-white hair that curled in a delightful fashion around her face. It was a pity she had to wear horn-rimmed glasses; they disfigured her.

"Yes, I do," she said.

"Did you know she was at the door?"

"No, I didn't hear anybody. I was singing, and Amelia's out."

"You're too kind to that girl. You let her go out too often."

"She does her work well, and we're only young once, you know," replied Mrs. Simpson, smiling.

"Yes, I suppose we are," agreed Jabez. "It was that Mrs. Trim at the door," he went on. "She comes to clean for Miss Merton, doesn't she?"

Mrs. Simpson carefully fixed a patch.

"Yes," she said, "twice a week."

"Is she crazy?" asked Jabez, standing, tall and thin as a barber's pole, by the lintel of the door.

"I should say she certainly isn't. Though she's had enough trouble to drive her crazy."

"Has she?" said Jabez indifferently. "Then, I think,

in spite of what you say, it must have affected her brain. She's been here and talked no end of rubbish. I couldn't make head or tail of it. Do you mind sending her away if she comes again."

"Very well," said Mrs. Simpson.

Jabez went back into the hall and down the short passage leading to his conservatory. As soon as he stepped into it he heaved a great sigh of contentment, and forgot all about Mrs. Trim and everybody else. For the roses that Jabez had in December were his joy and pride. They were no more lovely than roses that grow in June, but the fact that he—assisted by his gardener— grew them in December, when nobody else had any, gave Jabez peculiar satisfaction.

He had taken off his coat and rolled up his shirt sleeves ready to spray some of the blooms, when a door leading from the garden opened, and a small old lady limped in, tapping her way with a stick. She wore a black dress of ancient cut, but expensive material, an ugly, flat black hat, and an air of determination.

"Hullo!" said Jabez, going on with his work.

"'Hullo!' your grandmother," retorted his visitor. "Are you mad, Jabez?"

"Mad?" queried Jabez, pausing with one hand on a flower pot. "Why?"

Miss Merton lived next door to Jabez, and was an old lady of decided views that she never hesitated to state. "Don't be an idiot, Jabez," she said, "I mean Mrs. Trim."

Jabez put down the syringe he had been intending to use, and looked down at his neighbor like an eagle regarding a very impertinent sparrow.

"I haven't the faintest idea," he said, "what you're talking about. All I do know is that Mrs. Trim is crazy."

"If being crazy makes Mrs. Trim see 10 pound notes," replied Miss Merton, "then I dare say there are other people who would like to be crazy."

"If Mrs. Trim has seen 10 pound notes, I don't know what that has to do with me."

"Only that you gave them to her."

"I—gave—I—what?" stammered Jabez.

"Mrs. Trim received a registered envelope addressed in your writing, containing your name inside, and 10 pound notes, this morning. She rushed—"

Amelia opened the door.

"You're wanted on the phone, please, sir," she said.

"I can't come," snapped Jabez. "Take the message."

"The lady insists on speaking to you, sir."

"Go along, Jabez," suggested Miss Merton. "I'll come, and finish telling you after—hurry up!"

"Forgetting his coat, Jabez hurried into the hall, leaving Miss Merton to follow more slowly.

"Jabez Oldbury speaking," he barked into the receiver.

"Oh, Mr. Oldbury," came a feminine voice, "I really don't know how to thank you. You don't know what such a gift means at this time of the year."

"You've got the wrong number," said Jabez.

"You're Mr. Jabez Oldbury?"

"Yes—yes—but—"

"So sorry, there's a bad case just come in. I'm wanted. Many, many thanks."

Furiously, Jabez rang up the exchange, and found that it was the matron of a hospital who had been speaking to him.

"Now what's the matter?" demanded Miss Merton.

"I think," replied Jabez, "that there must be some escaped lunatics about today. That was somebody thanking me for something I don't know anything about—I don't even know what she was thanking me for, and whatever it was, I didn't do it."

"Of course you didn't," agreed Miss Merton.

"How do you know I didn't?" roared Jabez, angrily.

"You've just said you didn't, you old idiot," replied his neighbor calmly. "Besides, you wouldn't. You're not that sort."

"Well, now," said Jabez, "perhaps you'll be kind enough to finish telling me—"

"Excuse me, sir," remarked Amelia, appearing at that moment. "Sam Jackson's at the back door. He wants to speak to you."

"Sam Jackson? Who is Sam Jackson?" demanded Jabez, who by this time was getting really irritable.

"He keeps that little shop at the bottom of the lane, sir," replied Amelia.

"I'll wait," said little Miss Merton, and tapping her way into the dining room with her stick, she sat by the fire.

Jabez strode angrily to the back door. He was opening his mouth to growl at the man who stood there, when he noticed exactly the same expression in his eyes that had been in Mrs. Trim's, and Jabez could not say anything. He was acutely conscious of nothing but that wonderful look. He basked in it like a sun-starved child basking in the sun. In a half conscious fashion he heard the man thanking him for paying a doctor's bill of which he had never heard, but all Jabez wanted was that the man should go on looking at him for a long time. Jabez stammered something. Sam Jackson gripped his hand and walked away. In a half dazed fashion Jabez made his way back to the dining room and sank into the nearest chair.

"Well?" said Miss Merton.

"He wanted to thank me for paying a doctor's bill that I've never heard of," said Jabez.

"What did you say?"

"I . . . nothing . . . I . . ."

The front door bell rang. Without waiting for Amelia, and still without his coat, Jabez hurried to the door. Somebody had put a letter through the letter slot and it was on the floor. Jabez picked it up, and slit it open.

> "The Thatches.
> Dec. 20th.
>
> Dear Mr. Oldbury,
>   Many thanks for the lovely roses. God does indeed give us memory that we may have roses in December. I hope the December of your life may be filled with roses.
>   Yours very gratefully,
>   Sarah Spencer"

It was too much. His own gardener must have been giving away some of his beloved roses! Forgetting all about Miss Merton, Jabez dashed once more down the passage leading to the conservatory, and collided violently with a little man coming in the opposite direction. It was Ben, the gardener.

"Oh!" he gasped, clutching his nose, which was prominent, and had been nearly flattened.

"What do you mean by it?" roared Jabez.

"I couldn't 'elp it, sir. You was runnin' an' I was runnin' an—"

"What do you mean by giving away my roses, I mean?"

If Ben had been accused of giving away the clothes of his own body he could not have looked more astounded. "Why, sir," he gasped, "I'd sooner think o' flyin'." There was no doubt of Ben's innocence. He carried it on his face.

"And I was comin' to thank you, sir," he added.

"Thank me!" exclaimed Jabez. "Good gracious man, what for?"

"For the money for my new teeth."

"Money? Teeth? Come into the dining room and show me."

Ben followed his master, and from somewhere about his person he produced an envelope, addressed apparently by Jabez Oldbury, the envelope contained five pound notes, and the curt command written, again apparently by Ben's master, "Get some new teeth."

"These is always fallin' out, sir," remarked Ben, "an' I'm very much obliged to you. Teeth is awful expensive."

Before Jabez could recover from his astonishment, Ben had gone, and Miss Merton was showing her own excellent teeth in a wide smile.

"Read that," commanded Jabez, pushing the letter that he had found in the hall across the table.

Miss Merton read the note slowly.

"Christmas roses," she murmured, thoughtfully. "Jabez, there's somebody anxious to make out that you're everything you're not."

"What do you mean?" sputtered Jabez.

"Somebody is trying to make other people believe that you're kind and generous and Christmassy and all that sort of thing."

"And am I not?"

"Don't be a fool," snapped his neighbor. "You know you're not."

"Then why should anybody want to make out that I am?" asked Jabez, rubbing his bald head in a bewildered fashion.

"Goodness knows," replied Miss Merton. "That's what puzzles me. It's a waste of time and money, because you'll just go round to these people tomorrow and say you didn't do it, and that's that."

"What?" Jabez snapped out the word and closed his mouth like a rat trap.

He was thinking how hateful it would be to see that light go out of Mrs. Trim's eyes, out of Sam's eyes, and Ben's eyes.

"It's the only thing you can do," continued Miss Merton.

"Well . . . er . . . yes," stammered Jabez.

"You look like a worried walnut," remarked Miss Merton, "with your face all wrinkled up like that. Go and get your coat on."

"Sally," said Jabez, "did you do it?"

"Did I do what?"

"Did you give this money away in my name?"

"The person who did," replied Miss Merton, "is either a saint or a fool. I'm not sure which, and I'm neither. No, Jabez, I didn't. Put your coat on and walk across the garden with me."

The next morning there were six letters by the first post thanking Jabez for gifts of money about which he knew nothing. "Amelia," he said, "where does Mrs. Trim live?"

"Rose Cottage, sir."

Amelia was packing the breakfast things on a tray.

"What's been her trouble?" asked Jabez.

"Her husband was ill and out of work for months, then he died; and then Jim, her only boy, who was earning a few shillings a week, he got knocked down by a car and nearly killed. It never rains but it pours, sir."

"Seems like it," agreed Jabez. "My shoes clean?"

Jabez knocked at the door of Rose Cottage quite determined to tell Mrs. Trim the truth. As that lady opened the door, he opened his mouth, but the words he meant to say would not come. At sight of him that wonderful light leaped into Mrs. Trim's eyes, and Jabez could not put it out. Before he knew where he was he found himself in a spotless kitchen where a boy about 16 sat by the fire.

"Here's Mr. Oldbury, Jim," said Mrs. Trim.

Jim blushed and stammered.

Jabez blushed and stammered.

Mrs. Trim came to the rescue by remarking, "He'll be able to go away now, sir, your money'll cure him."

"You'll go too, of course?" said Jabez, recovering a little.

"Me? No, sir. The money'll keep one person away longer than two."

Jabez drew what Mrs. Trim afterward called "a queer book" from his pocket, wrote in it, tore out a paper, handed it to her, growled, "Take that to the bank. They'll give you some money. You go away, too."

Before the astonished woman, or her son, could recover, Jabez had fallen over the cat; kicked over the milk jug that stood on the step; and was flying down the lane as though pursued by demons, but feeling a strange happiness he had never known before.

He went to Sam Jackson's shop, and when he left he knocked over a bottle of pickled onions that stood on the counter, and kicked a box of eggs from one end of the shop to the other, but he left behind a check and two very grateful hearts, one belonging to Sam, the other to his wife. When Jabez got home, Miss Merton was waiting for him.

"Well?" she said.

"Well?" replied Jabez.

"You told them?"

"No, I didn't."

"What?" Miss Merton peered over the top of her glasses.

"I didn't, I said."

"Then what did you say?" demanded Miss Merton. "You know Mrs. Trim chars for me. She'll tell me, if you don't."

"Let her tell you, then," replied Jabez. "I'm going to see Mrs. Spencer."

Mrs. Spencer was an invalid, but she was not poor. In her room Jabez found a bunch of exquisite roses, and beside them a Christmas card, with another bunch of roses, and the words "God gives us memory, that we may have roses in December."

"I liked the card," said Mrs. Spencer, "as much as the flowers."

"The words are beautiful," agreed Jabez, not really thinking of them, but wondering where those lovely blooms could have come from, and while he was wondering, Mrs. Spencer was talking—

"It's a beautiful idea," she was saying, "and there are other roses for December besides sweet memories, and memories of kind deeds aren't there?"

"Are there?" Jabez was still thinking of the real roses.

"Well, my children are my December roses," replied the invalid. "What should I do now—in the December of my life without them?"

Jabez started like a man walking from a dream. Once he had been in love, but not even for love had Jabez been prepared to take any risks. He hadn't, he thought at that time, enough money to marry. So little Ann, with her dark, curling hair, her gray eyes that were like sea seen through mist, had faded out of his life.

"I—never thought of children like that," he stammered. "I always thought of them as—well—a responsibility—a burden."

"Their backs are strong when ours are weak. I shouldn't have mentioned it if you hadn't sent me these roses. I'm sorry if I've touched a tender spot."

"You've only made me realize what a fool I've been," growled Jabez. Then, as he stumbled in his usual clumsy way out of the house, he added, "I'll send some more roses."

Miss Merton was watching from her window for

Jabez, and as he passed she beckoned to him to come in. "Well," she said, "did you find out anything?"

"Yes," snapped Jabez.

"What?" barked the little old lady, sitting up suddenly like a Jack-in-the-box.

"That I'm a fool."

"My dear man, I mean something I didn't know. Why, I've been telling you that for years. Did you find out who the Christmas rose person is?"

"No, I didn't."

Miss Merton peered at Jabez over her glasses. "Do you know," she said, "what I should think if it weren't too absurd? I should think if I didn't know it was impossible, that there's somebody who loves you."

"Don't be a . . . don't be funny," growled Jabez.

"Don't mind what you call me," said Miss Merton, knitting busily. "If you're rude to me I can always be rude to you."

Jabez grinned broadly. "I know you can," he said.

"My dear old idiot," went on the old lady, "some wise person has managed to make you realize that you're missing a lot in life—you've always snapped my head off if I tried to tell you. I suppose I've gone the wrong way about it; you'll find when December comes that you'll wish you'd grown more Christmas roses, I know."

Jabez stood over the fireplace.

"I know. I've seen Mrs. Trim."

"I've started to grow them," he growled.

Suddenly Miss Merton leaned across and put a withered hand on Jabez's knee. "Take my advice," she said, "don't rest till you find out who's done it."

Then she stood up and patted the bald spot on his head. "Good night, Jabez," she said.

"Good night, Sally," he replied, getting up to open the door for her.

The earth was covered with white frost and a big round moon rode in a cloudless sky as Jabez made his way over his neighbor's garden into his own. It was very late when he went to bed that night, and it was not until he was undressing that he missed a small notebook from his pocket. It must have slipped out when he took his coat off in the greenhouse, things often did.

He put on his dressing gown and crept down to get it. The conservatory was flooded with moonlight, and Jabez easily found the book, then he stood still breathing the perfume of the roses, looking at the garden asleep under its white blanket of frost. Sound itself was sleeping, and Jabez almost held his breath.

Suddenly his tall figure straightened. Out of the shadows that surrounded his own house a figure appeared; a small figure covered in something dark, and silent as the night. One hand clutched the cloak so that it should not open, and the same hand held a bunch of—Jabez stared—they looked like—they were— roses. As Jabez opened the greenhouse door the latch clicked; the little figure turned sharply, gasped, and stood still. So did Jabez.

They stood in perfect silence with the moonlight all about them, gazing at one another. Then Jabez stooped, blinked, like somebody who cannot believe what he sees, and looked more closely. Two gray eyes like the sea seen through mist never flinched as he stared into them.

"Ann," he just breathed the little name. "Ann—it

can't be—Ann—Mrs. Simpson."

"My hair has gone white, you see, Jabez, and I wore glasses so that you shouldn't know me. Twenty years is a long time. I was always good at housekeeping, so I chose to earn—to work that way."

"You're a widow then?"

Ann shook her head. "I'm Ann Anderson, as I always was."

"Mrs. Simpson?"

"It was easy to get a friend to do all that, Jabez, to give me a reference and put that name in it. Somebody who knew us both in the old days told me you were living here, and you needed a housekeeper, and—and—all about you."

"And these?" Jabez touched the roses.

Ann hesitated for the first time. "These," she said, "are from—I've hidden them. Amelia's never seen them. And I imitated your writing well, didn't I?"

"Where have they come from?" insisted Jabez.

"They're from my own hothouses."

Jabez gasped. "Your own hothouse? And you've been working as my housekeeper."

Ann nodded, and at the door of Jabez's memory there hammered the words Miss Merton had said that very day—there must be somebody who loves you."

Jabez reached out two long arms, and put his hands on Ann's shoulders. He turned so that the moonlight fell full upon her face, and the black cloak slipped from her lovely, ruffled hair.

"Why?" he demanded mercilessly. "Why, Ann?"

Her gray eyes never flinched from his.

"You've got everything in life that matters second, Jabez; I wanted you to have everything that matters first. I wanted you to see gratitude in people's eyes; to hear it in their voices. I wanted you to have some roses for December—you've missed some, you know."

"It's worse than that, Ann," he said. "I've made you miss some."

"Yes," she admitted, "you have."

"Ann," said Jabez, "I've been a fool. The biggest fool ever created. If I waited a long time could you ever bring yourself to forgive me, and to help me to grow a few December roses?"

Ann was not looking at him now; her eyes were fixed on the roses in her hand, and she was very quiet.

"Never mind, dear," said Jabez. "I oughtn't to have said it. It was like my cheek."

Then the two gray eyes, full of laughter and tears, were lifted: "I was thinking," said Ann, "that as you're 50 and I'm 40, it's a pity to wait."

Luther

Joe L. Wheeler
as told by
Michelle Wheeler Culmore

Two Christmases ago, my daughter Michelle first told me the story of Luther. It is a story that has refused to go away. We humans are so glib about the taking of life. Not just human life but animal and bird as well. But the Creator, in His great wisdom, put each one of them on this planet for a reason. A reason my daughter now understands.

I tried, in its retelling, to preserve the natural rhythm of my daughter's original narrative. It is told simply, naturally, just as she remembers it.

Actually, it was a miracle that I ever met Luther, because he had been bought earlier in the fall to fatten up for Thanksgiving dinner. But something happened along the way to give him a Hezekiah reprieve: they fell in love with him—to have eaten him would have been like eating one of the family!

So partly at least, to get him out of temptation's way, he was delivered to the theater to begin his dramatic career.

A senior fashion major, I was interning in a New England public theater, cutting my teeth—and other body parts—on costume design and repair.

Having always yearned to be in New England in the fall—*and* in the winter—the opportunity seemed almost too good to be true. When I arrived, it was to the lazy, hazy days of late summer when the heat slows life down to a catlike slouch. But before long, the cooler winds of autumn swept down from Canada, and all nature came alive again.

Soon it was "peak," as the natives label it, and all across New England the leaves turned to scarlet, orange, amber, and gold. Their reflection in the sky blue of the lakes and rivers took one's breath away. And spearing through the rainbow of colors were the soaring spires of blinding white churches, legacy of those intrepid Puritans, three and three quarters centuries ago.

And then came Luther.

They sent him to stay at the theater for the remainder of the fall season. He came with his snow-white feathers and in a small cage with some plain, dried food and a water dish. Not knowing what else to do with him, he was hauled down to the theater basement with the unwarranted assumption that the stage manager, Torsten, would somehow take care of him.

The theater basement was one of the places I hated the most. It was very, *very*, **very** dirty, damp, dark, and unorganized. I can't even *begin* to describe how dirty it was. Sort of a dumping ground for the theater: stage supplies, props, tools, trash, and remnants of the theater itself were strewn all over. And like most New England buildings, it had been there a long, long time. It was even said that there was a resident ghost. If true, it surely slept a lot, because no one I knew had ever seen it. Nor did I.

The basement was under the theater itself, but was not paved or floored. It was essentially gravel, rocks, loose rusty nails, cement chunks, and who knows what else. One never went down there without heavy shoes on. When I remembered—and could find one—I'd wear a mask. Heaven only knows what toxic chemicals (asbestos, etc.) were staining the air—and it was grossly filthy to boot. Every time I went down, within an hour or so, I'd get a headache, feel like I was coming down with a cold, and get a runny nose. And the grime in the air would rain down on body and clothes; in no time at all, you were filthy—inside and out.

I have to give Torsten credit, however. He did his best to fix it up during those rare occasions when he had spare time. As foul as it was, it was said to be an improvement on his predecessor's subterranean junkyard, one strata down.

Needless to say, imagine what all this did to the beautiful, clean goose—stuck down there for more than a month! In no time at all, he had lost his shimmering white beauty and had turned an ugly, grimy gray. And his health obviously suffered as well.

As if these conditions and the intermittent darkness were not enough, there were the kids—all 150 of them—streaming downstairs in hordes in order to get measured for their "Christmas Carol" costuming. They needed that many because there were two children's casts and a month-long run; out of the 150, they hoped 50 a night would actually show up.

Unfortunately, we could only process them a few at a time—and that left them with time on their hands. To no one's surprise, they didn't wait well. In fact, it was bedlam! Just the memory of it gives me a headache.

Worse yet, it didn't take them long to discover Luther. They took turns playing with him, teasing him, taunting him, mistreating him. Amazingly, not once did he use that sharp beak of his to strike back. He just took it.

The staff wasn't much help either. Quite frankly, they were ticked that this unexpected responsibility had been thrust upon them. A not unsurprising response given the fact that they were all overworked and underpaid—if paid at all.

So . . . Luther quacked and pooped (green, by the way) all the time—most likely because he was in goose hell and yearned to get out.

I suppose he became attached to me because I was the one around the most and consequently paid the most attention to him. I ended up being the one who fed and watered him most of the time. At that time, we were in the concluding days of "Othello" and frantically—simultaneously, of course!—preparing for "Christmas Carol."

Luther detested his cage and used his canny mind to the fullest in figuring out ways to ditch it. As a result, he got out often. And when he didn't get out on his own, the kids *helped!* During one of these escapes, he cut one of his webbed feet on a rusty nail. Fortunately, Tracey (one of the actresses) had previously worked for a veterinarian. She was the only one (other than me, and later on, Jay—head costumer and actor) sympathetic to Luther's plight.

We dug up some first aid stuff and tried to clean up his poor foot—no easy task when the grimy sink appears to never have been washed itself. There was nothing clean down there to ever set such a precedent! Then, we put him in the shower (disgustingly dirty, too, but the "cleanest" alternative around), and Tracey, costume, stage makeup, and all, got in with him. I locked the bathroom door (to keep kids and others out) and joined her in the cleaning process.

Unfortunately, she forgot she was supposed to go on stage when she was "called," nor was I there to help with last-minute costume changes and alterations, etc. The play went on without us (luckily for her, in that scene she was only an extra). But later on, the director added a scene not in the script when he tracked us down after the curtain call.

Anyway, we used soap and shampoo to clean Luther up, feather by feather, layer by layer. He adjusted to this tripartite shower with such nonchalance one would have thought such strange doings were part of his normal routine. We were a little apprehensive about what effect shampoo might have on the natural oil in his feathers, but concluded that few alternatives were worse than his current state. We then toweled him off (a process that gradually revealed light-gray feathers), cleaned, disinfected, and wrapped up his foot as best we could, taped it, and he was free to try and walk. He was very cheerful about it all—except for the dubious looks he gave our bandaging artistry—and began cleaning his feathers.

The next morning, he was white again.

And so Luther and I became friends.

Once he got to know me, he adored my petting him. He was most inquisitive, always wanting to know what was going on. Had he been a cat, he would have been purring on my lap; being a goose, he took second best and enthroned himself on the floor beneath my sewing machine.

And he was *very* vocal. I'd love to have a transcript decoding his end of our long talks together.

The bandage kept coming off—or snipped off, we never knew which—but we tried to monitor his recovery as best we could. He'd get dirty again and again and again. I tried to keep him with me as much as possible, but it was difficult—and more than a little annoying—as what went in one end promptly came out the other. In a steady stream. He never seemed to feel the need to wait for a "more convenient season," consequently I was continually cleaning up behind him, feeling much like a circus lady with a shovel in the wake of an elephant. Disgusting! Nevertheless, the process didn't seem to humiliate *him!* He followed me around everywhere I went in those downstairs catacombs, quacking indignantly as if to say, "Hey! Where do you think you're going? Wait up!"

As the "Christmas Carol" marathon began gathering speed and my work accelerated at an ever faster pace, I moved my ironing board, sewing machine, etc. over to the theater basement and into the backstage makeup room. Luther thought he had died and gone to heaven when I moved him in, too, to keep me company. Maintaining sideways eye contact (goose fashion), he quacked away with his stories hour after hour, only stopping once in a while to take a nap.

Then, as we neared zero hour, I worked there with Luther virtually around the clock, till I was hard-pressed to avoid falling asleep at my sewing machine. Every once in a while, I'd shake myself awake again, only to look down and see Luther eyeing me with puzzled concern and quacking solace.

Opening night came at last, but by this time I was almost too tired to care. Everyone else, however, was illuminated by that inner excitement which always accompanies first night performances. Rumor was that a big-time city critic was going to be there, which added an extra edge to the excitement.

Soon I could hear the crowd upstairs. The milling around. The voices. And then the clapping. And after all the work I had done, I wasn't even able to sit back in the auditorium and enjoy seeing my handiwork. Here I was, still sewing, still altering, still helping to salvage or repair garments during and after each scene. Before the winter street scenes, it was a madhouse putting mittens, hats, coats, and mufflers on all the fidgety children before their entrances onstage. As an added treat, just before the biggest scene, one frightened little girl, overwhelmed by stage fright, threw up on half a dozen costumes we had spent so much time mending, cleaning, and ironing. This created an even madder rush to find more costumes to replace them.

And then it was finally time for the big street scene, when Dickens' London was reproduced in all its vitality and diversity: with 50 children—all behaving now, wide-eyed and innocent—with several pet dogs and a pet ferret (one previous year, there had been a horse!). The entire cast was onstage at the same time . . . and Luther.

125

So it was that long before Tiny Tim's piping, "God bless us. Every one!" would bring that beloved story full circle, Luther had celebrated his acting debut by waddling across the stage. Noting how frightened he looked, Jay leaned down and picked him up. Tenderly cradling his feathered (white again) body in his arms, and feeling the tom-tom of his fast-beating heart. From that refuge, Luther contentedly looked out over the delighted audience, and quacked out a soft "Hello."

Sadly, I was not able to stay for the rest of the run. In all my last-minute packing and bequeathing of responsibilities, however, one worry remained constant: *After I am gone, what will happen to poor Luther?* We moved his cage to a far corner of the basement (actually, into Torsten's office). There was thus a cement floor and a door we could shut (1) to try and keep the kids from tormenting him and (2) to keep his lonely

squawks from disturbing the audience. This room was much, much better than the first. But there he was, left alone. I felt terribly guilty every time I shut that door and heard him entreating me to come back.

As the last moments of my tenure at the theater trickled down like sand in the hourglass of my life, Luther began squawking nonstop. Actually, "squawking" is a totally inadequate word for what I heard. There is no one word in the dictionary that can begin to capture it; the closest I can come to is that it was halfway between an outraged squawk and a heartbroken sob. There was absolutely no question in my mind: he *knew!* Even though Jay promised to take care of him, I knew it would never be the same. It was heart-wrenching. It was terrible!

All the way back to Maryland I could hear him cry: "Why, why did you forsake me? *Why?*"

I still hear him. . . . In sleepless nights. . . . In restless days. . . . How this one little goose—nothing but soiled, once-white feathers, two inquisitive eyes, a quacking story that never quite got told, and a heart as big as all New England—could make such a difference in this hectic life I live, I guess I'll never understand. It just has.

That Christmas, Jay, bless him!—knowing I'm such a sentimental ol' fool—sent me a present. It was small, and my fingers shook a little as I opened it. It was a lovely ceramic ornament. One side was flat. But the other—the other side featured, in relief, a white bird. A goose. Luther!